MAKING TIME

Also by William L. Fox

Nonfiction
Driving to Mars
Terra Antarctica: Looking into the Emptiest Continent
In the Desert of Desire: Las Vegas and the Culture of Spectacle
Playa Works: The Myth of the Empty Universe
The Black Rock Desert
Viewfinder: Mark Klett and the Reinvention of Landscape Photography
The Void, the Grid, & the Sign: Traversing the Great Basin
Driving by Memory
Mapping the Empty: Eight Artists and Nevada

Poetry
Reading Sand: Selected Desert Poems, 1976–2000
One Wave Standing
silence and license
geograph
Leaving Elko
Time by Distance
21 and Over
The Yellow Pages
First Principles
Monody
Election
Trial Separation
Iron Wind

MAKING TIME

ESSAYS ON THE NATURE OF LOS ANGELES

William L. Fox

[signature]

06/08

shoemaker **S&H** hoard

Library of Congress Cataloging-in-Publication Data

Fox, William L., 1949–
Making time : essays on the nature of Los Angeles / William L. Fox.
p. cm.
Includes bibliographical references
ISBN-13: 978-1-59376-133-2 (alk. paper)
ISBN-10: 1-59376-133-3 (alk. paper)
1. Los Angeles (Calif.)—Civilization. 2. Los Angeles
(Calif.)—Geography. 3. Los Angeles (Calif.)—Description and travel.
4. Time—Social aspects—California—Los Angeles. 5. Cognition and
culture—California—Los Angeles. 6. Landscape—Social
aspects—California—Los Angeles. 7. Motion picture industry—Social
aspects—California—Los Angeles. 8. Fox, William L.,
1949– —Travel—California—Los Angeles. 9. Los Angeles
(Calif.)—Environmental conditions. I. Title.

F869.L85F695 2006
979.4'94—dc22

2006030691

Cover design by Gerilyn Attebery
Interior design by David Bullen
Printed in the United States of America

Shoemaker & Hoard
An Imprint of Avalon Publishing Group, Inc.

AVALON

1400 65th Street, Suite 250
Emeryville, CA 94608
Distributed by Publishers Group West

10 9 8 7 6 5 4 3 2 1

for Karen

CONTENTS

MAKING TIME

TRACKING TAR

It was the volcano emerging from the lake at the end of the street that finally did it. Earlier in the day, finding myself restless and unable to concentrate, I'd taken a walk over to the La Brea Tar Pits to meditate on the methane bubbles that rise lugubriously up through the water. I circumambulated the twenty-six acres of the park in a clockwise direction, against the flow of the elementary- and middle-school students being herded by their teachers, and paused to lean on handrails to watch tourists pitch lit cigarettes at the three-foot-wide burps.

A by-product of bacteria eating up vegetative matter, methane is the predominant component of natural gas and is often associated with oil. It's an odorless, colorless, and relatively stable gas, which is a good thing, considering the well-aimed cigarettes. Nothing ignited on the tar pit that day, as the gas disperses too quickly, but when concentrated in small places and mixed with air, as transpired in the basement of a nearby department store on March 24, 1985, methane explodes rather nicely. Fortunately, no one was in the basement of Ross Dress for Less when it blew, the building rising just slightly with an enormous burp, then settling back down, although twenty-two people were injured. Shortly thereafter, management sealed the foundation and vented the basement; you can see the pipes at the back of the building. They elevate the gas to roof level, where it wafts harmlessly away over the parking lot.

The gas bubbles in the viscous water at the tar pits were, as always, moderately chaotic in their behavior. They rise from vents underneath a large pond of accumulated groundwater that has filled in an asphalt quarry dug in the nineteenth century. The gas roils the surface into a yellow-green froth; large ripples subside quickly on the oil-slicked surface and barely reach the shore. So when, after returning home and eating dinner, I watched a video of glowing lava push its way up into the middle of the lake and begin oozing down Wilshire Boulevard, I'd been both surprised and not. After all, I was living in an active seismic zone over an oil field, and not atop a volcanic vent, two very different kinds of geological structures. On the other hand, after having watched the movie crews a few months earlier drape the nearby multistoried Beverly Center shopping mall with plastic in preparation for shooting the street scenes in *Volcano,* it was almost anticlimactic. Let me explain.

I was living in Park La Brea, a seventy-five-acre development of townhouses and apartment towers built in the 1940s. The development holds upward of eight thousand residents, median age currently around thirty-two. Because it was designed by a French architect, it has a radial street design instead of a rectilinear one like the rest of L.A. If it weren't for the fact that my street therefore ran southwest instead of south or west, I wouldn't have been able to see Hancock Park and the George C. Page Museum from my front door. Consequently, I wouldn't have been so inclined to walk out the Park La Brea gate and cross the street to the tar pits, as I had in midafternoon. And perhaps watching the movie *Volcano* that evening, a highly improbable 1997 disaster flick from Twentieth Century Fox, wouldn't have struck me as an epiphany that started this book.

Sitting through movies in L.A. can be trying. First of all,

many of my neighbors in the complex worked in or were close to the movie business. I was living adjacent to the offices of the Screen Actors Guild, and I often encountered waiflike young actresses, many of whom lived in or near Park La Brea, walking down the sidewalk reading scripts out loud to themselves. E! Entertainment was two blocks south, as was the trade rag *Variety*, and the CBS studios were only two blocks north.

Everywhere you drove in the neighborhood, movies were being made, the traffic diverted or held back by motorcycle cops assigned to steer people away from the lights and trailers and thick bundles of cable. So many film crews work a few blocks east in residential Hancock Park, where various houses stand in for Chicago, Boston, and other eastern American locations, that the local homeowners' association continually registers protests with the studios, the police, the city council, and anyone else it thinks might listen. In a town where a sizable chunk of the civic economy is tied up in the business, however, there's not much of a sympathetic audience. Part of the reason is that the studios pay handsome fees to the owners of the houses they rent—fees that help the homeowners pay their sky-high property taxes in one of America's ten most expensive neighborhoods.

The film industry is so pervasive in Park La Brea and environs that when you first sit down with your neighbors to watch a television show or a movie, you soon realize that they're not as interested in the story as in who's playing whom. They're looking for friends, people they've worked with, or actors who have beaten them out for parts, or they're simply keeping up with business. In theaters frequented by people who work in the movies, audiences sit patiently through the entirety of the ever-longer credits to acknowledge with applause the work of their friends and enemies, a ceremonial behavior that for all

I know goes back to spectators in the Colosseum of ancient Rome.

Even those Angelenos not involved with the business pay more attention than do people elsewhere in the world to movie sets and locations, learning how to distinguish which parts of, say, New York are actually filmed on the Paramount back lot and which are filmed on the real streets of the Big Apple. It's a logical outcome of living in the middle of what in the twentieth century became the world's largest movie set: Parts of the Los Feliz neighborhood stand in for Tuscany; Pasadena substitutes for Cuba; City Hall becomes Gotham City.

So it was with mixed amazement and bemusement that I sat watching a video of lava pour down a street a block and a half away, which is to say, three-quarters of a mile along a Wilshire Boulevard and from a volcano re-created at seven-eighths scale on a gigantic parking lot in Torrance. Apart from the incorrect premise that a volcano would push its way up through the middle of L.A., and the movie's at-best skimpy plot, the production team actually got the eruption down pretty well. The special-effects people studied films of lava, built a table-top version of Wilshire, and rolled a variety of goos down the fake street until they got a substance that looked realistic when filmed at that miniature scale. What finally worked best was a concoction of methylcellulose, a wood industry by-product used to thicken milkshakes by certain fast-food chains that shall remain nameless, and pigments that fluoresced when lit with ultraviolet lights, thus glowing like embers.

Twentieth Century Fox received the largest fire permit ever issued to a movie set to stage *Volcano*, a construction project that took three to four hundred people more than 132,000 work-hours to complete. Add 150,000 gallons of liquid propane, 2,500 pounds of explosives, and 250 tons of shredded paper to stand in for ash, and you have eruptions, lava, and a volcanic dandruff that settled nicely on the shoulders of Tommy Lee Jones and Anne Heche as they stumbled past the seven-eighths-scale model of the Los Angeles County Museum of Art.

So here we had $100 million being spent to simulate a natural disaster, and actors running away from a theoretical stream of approaching lava that they couldn't even see, the miniature shots of the supposedly molten rock computer-enhanced and edited in later. And there I was, sitting at home with people who were parsing out how it was all done with smoke and mirrors, the current legal status of Tommy Lee Jones, the romantic lesbian entanglements of Ms. Heche, and how the crew even faked exactly right the art deco facade of the May Building. It occurred to me that the reality of the La Brea Tar Pits might be more interesting and disturbing than the fictional volcano. This idea might be a way to decipher how nature and culture coexist both in L.A. and, increasingly, in the minds of people around the world, since film culture is the predominant planetwide visual entertainment of human beings.

The La Brea Tar Pits sit at the southern edge of what's called the Salt Lake Field, a relatively small sandstone reservoir from which oil is pumped at several locations, including a fenced and unobtrusive well station on the northeast corner of the Farmers Market near the CBS studios. There's a theory that petroleum is a much more plentiful resource than we once thought, that hydrocarbons exist very deep in the planet and rise continually toward the surface, constantly replenishing oil fields around the world. Thomas Gold, the noted astrophysicist who correctly predicted in 1957 that the moon was covered with dust and not with hardened lava (the prevailing theory of the time), was the principal author of this theory. He pointed out that hydrocarbons have been detected on Titan, a moon of Saturn. Oil on the earth is commonly known to be mostly a by-product of organic decay, primarily of plankton that died in ancient oceans during the Miocene epoch from 5 to 25 million years ago. Plankton, the free-floating, unicellular animal and plant life that makes up the majority of the biomass on the planet, sinks to the ocean floor when the organisms die. Over unimaginably long periods, this deposition is layered with sand and compressed into oil.

No plankton has ever existed on either Titan or the other planets and moons in our solar system, yet we've detected large quantities of hydrocarbons and methane on them. Gold postulated that hydrocarbons are pervasive in other members of the solar system because the chemicals are a by-product of planetary formation. We drill for oil only three or four miles down. Gold said there are reserves as deep as two hundred miles in the earth, and that internal pressures within the planet will eventually drive them upward. If we're patient, he argued, wells that have run dry will refill and keep refilling for thousands of years. Although most scientists disagree with Gold's theory or think the deep hydrocarbons might be too dispersed to be captured easily, Russia has been producing oil from three hundred wells drilled straight into bedrock. According to prevailing wisdom, this is impossible—unless Gold's theory is correct, or some other explanation arises.

All this is of some amusement to Hal Washburn, one of the owners of BreitBurn Energy Corporation, a company that pumps oil out of the Salt Lake Field. Washburn, who cofounded in 1989 what is now one of California's largest independent oil companies, graduated from Stanford University with a bachelor of science degree in petroleum engineering. He then worked as a managing engineer with another large independent outfit before teaming up with his former classmate, Randall Breitenbach, to start the company. They realized while still in undergraduate school that the massive computing power formerly available only to multinational oil conglomerates, such as ARCO and Shell, which were using Cray supercomputers to crunch geological data in search of oil, was now available in the personal computers sitting on their desktops.

The average amount of oil recovered from a field is traditionally only around 20 percent of what's actually in the ground, the rest being too difficult and expensive to recover with simple pumping. The two men thought that by using computers to more accurately model the fields, and by recirculating back into the ground the water that's invariably pumped out with the oil, they could constantly repressurize the field and squeeze it a bit harder and thereby retrieve 3 percent more petroleum. Applying their method would demand a certain scale of operations if it were to be cost-effective, however. The recovery of 3 percent of a field with only a few hundred thousand barrels in reserve, even at the then-current price of twenty dollars a barrel, wouldn't be profitable. On the other hand, 3 percent of a field pumping millions of barrels would be. The trick would be to find large enough fields with existing wells that they could lease.

Washburn and Breitenbach chose Los Angeles as the base for their operations because it has dozens of proven oil fields with existing infrastructure for which production could be enhanced with their methods and because its fields are among the largest in the country. Taking over oil fields on the west side of L.A. from Occidental Petroleum, which, like the other big companies of the region, pulled out when oil prices fell sharply in the late

1980s, they were soon pumping up 50 percent more oil than the former owners had been when they quit.

"L.A. is the richest oil basin in North America, and the second richest in the world," Washburn said, as he unpinned a large map from his wall and spread it over his desk between us. Around six feet tall, tan, and with a short beard going gray, Washburn was dressed in khakis and a plaid shirt, looking like a man who would rather be outside than in an office tower near the intersection of two freeways on the border of Santa Monica.

"Here are the major fields in the basin. Los Angeles has five out of the ten top fields in the country. See this one, the Wilmington Field?" he asked, pointing to a long, green blob stretching from Long Beach to Redondo. "That's a billion barrels. And this one over here, that's half a billion. So's this one." The fields were grouped irregularly around two converging axes, two fault zones. One ran northwest from Newport Beach to Inglewood, and the other, actually a series of associated faults, tended more northerly, from Santa Fe Springs through downtown, then bent west to run along the foot of the Santa Monica Mountains, which define the northwestern edge of the basin.

Reinhard Suchland, a compact and quiet man who is the company's manager of geology, joined us, adding, "The ground here is very petroliferous, the oil only five to ten million years old and, in strata, fifteen to twenty million years old. It's pretty young oil." Suchland was so matter-of-fact that even his characterizing ten-million-year-old oil as young sounded reasonable, yet I had the eerie feeling that my assumptions about time were soon going to slide over an unexpected cliff.

Washburn had taken the opportunity to slip out to the conference room. He returned bearing a large, framed print of an old photo showing the Salt Lake Field early in the twentieth century. "The early fields were found in the nineteenth century by surface features, like the tar seeps at La Brea. Here's Wilshire Boulevard; look at this, there's a well on every five acres, at least."

I peered at the black-and-white photograph of the area, trying to locate where Park La Brea now sat, and where, two and one-half miles to the east, my great-grandmother had built her house in Hancock Park in 1924. The derricks would have been taken down by then, as the development was being platted, but she and J. Paul Getty were building their houses across from each other on a street paved over a barely reclaimed oil field. Getty moved to Los Angeles in 1916 after buying and selling oil field leases in Tulsa with his father. He later ran the Getty Oil Company, which was bought by Texaco in 1984. A billionaire at the time of his death, he was reputed to be the richest man in the world, due in no small part to oil rights he controlled in the Middle East.

In 1859, a whale-oil merchant had sneaked onto Major Henry Hancock's Rancho La Brea property and set up a still to produce liquid asphalt from the seeps around the tar pits. Hancock chased him off, but the major's son, Captain George Hancock, operated a commercial asphalt operation there from 1870 to 1890. The earliest oil well in California was drilled in Newhall, north of the San Fernando Valley, in 1865, only six years after the first one in Pennsylvania, but it wasn't until 1876 that commercial oil was produced in California. The company setting up the commercial production would become the Standard Oil Company of California. Edward Doheny's discovery of oil in downtown Los Angeles set off a genuine boom in 1892; within five years, the city had five hundred derricks. The truly

giant fields in the Los Angeles Basin were struck in Huntington
Beach in 1920 and then under Santa Fe Springs and Signal Hill
the next year.

According to the California Department of Conservation's
Division of Oil, Gas, and Geothermal Resources, by 1998,
about 170,000 oil, gas, and geothermal wells had been drilled
in California; roughly 86,000 of them were still active, run by
seven hundred companies. A total of 46,434 oil wells were being
operated in the state, some by companies owning no more than
one or two wells. Washburn, who estimated that there were
probably more than a hundred oil companies presently pumping in L.A., told me of one local operation that consisted of a
ninety-year-old woman who owned a couple of wells in her
backyard. She had inherited them from her husband, and she
still operated them single-handedly. In 1998, more than 5 million feet of drilling took place statewide, with more than 2,100
new wells completed, but at the same time, 1,423 were plugged
and abandoned, a tally that rolled over annually, according to
the profitability of pumping at each site.

"California produces just under a million barrels of oil a
day, about half of what we use in the state. The rest comes in
by tanker trucks, ships, and trains," Washburn told me, sitting
down after propping up the Wilshire photo next to a wall. "It's
safer to produce it here than bring it in from elsewhere. I mean,
remember the *Exxon Valdez*?" He let the question hang in the
air. "But it's risky, exploring for oil. The old rule of thumb is
that you bring in one out of every ten wells you drill; with all
our new technology over the last hundred years, we've increased
that to maybe one in eight.

"All the big companies are mostly out of L.A. now, con-
solidating their operations, which I think we'll see more of in

the future. To give you a comparison, the L.A. Basin produces about thirty-eight million barrels of oil a year. Outside Bakersfield in the San Joaquin Valley, they're producing two hundred and fifty million barrels. We're a niche company, competing by using cutting-edge technology and keeping our overhead low." And, in fact, the heaps of packing boxes around us were evidence of that. Located on Sepulveda on the far west side of L.A., BreitBurn had seen rents double recently due to the influx of dot-com businesses. The company was getting ready to move downtown, taking advantage of Class A office space vacated, ironically, by ARCO as the larger company pulled its headquarters out of town.

Then it was Reinhard's turn to bring in a piece of show-and-tell. He set in my hand a heavy semicircle of dark, grainy core about four inches long and almost as wide. "That's part of a sandstone core from forty-eight hundred seventy-five feet down," he said. "It's been squeezed by overburden, and it's full of oil."

Its heft was unexpected in my palm. Looking at the grain, I'd expected the much lighter weight of regular sandstone, which is usually less compressed and not filled with petroleum. I brought it up to my nose and immediately smelled the engine of every car I'd ever owned, from a Volkswagen Bug in 1967 to my Honda in the parking lot next door. It made me think of cruising Virginia Street during high school in Reno on Friday nights, a sensory memory so loaded with nostalgia that it made me want to lick the dense and faintly striated core. I resisted with difficulty, but continued to hold the sandstone sample that was perhaps twenty million years old and from almost a mile down in the earth. Again, time was doing funny things in my head, an ancient geological sample throwing me back more than thirty years in my own life. The core evoked time as a visceral experience, not as a science lecture.

"The last significant onshore drilling in the basin around where you live was done in the sixties and seventies," Washburn said, continuing his history lesson. "The Beverly Hills Field was being drilled then. The Salt Lake Field, like others, was consolidated, most of the derricks taken down. What you do now is slant drilling from an existing well off at an angle to tap into new, usually deeper oil-bearing strata. That Farmers Market site has twenty wells operating there. It's not got a lot of oil left, maybe twenty or thirty years' worth, depending on the price."

I was amazed at this, having walked nonchalantly through the gate at the site a couple of weeks before, finding the entryway unexpectedly open when I was driving around to locate wells near Park La Brea. I'd counted what I thought were a maximum of six wells, just humps of yellow pipes and valves set relatively low to the ground, before sticking my head in the manager's office and starting to ask questions. I had startled the two men inside, who obviously weren't expecting visitors and who politely but firmly noted I was trespassing and that I should contact the corporate offices if I had any questions. They gave me the phone number that led me to Washburn and his geologist, watched carefully as I left, then closed and locked the gate behind me. Another well-hunting trip the same week had led me to the Beverly Center, the behemoth mall located about a mile west of the La Brea Tar Pits. At the parking entrance facing Beverly Hills sat an active drilling rig, the only oil well I know of at a shopping mall. I hadn't realized that it was tapped into the west end of the same field, until Washburn mentioned it.

I was beginning to realize that what Hal Washburn saw as

a small field was actually several square miles in extent. And while I conceived of it in terms of two-dimensional acreage, he was describing it in three dimensions of planetary volume and barrels in reserve.

"I don't think there will be much more development now in the basin," said Washburn. He rose from his chair to contemplate the map on his desk. "See these gaps in between the fields?" He pointed at the chain of rough oblongs stretching west underneath the southern edge of the Hollywood Hills and Santa Monica Mountains, then in between the Salt Lake, the South Salt Lake, and the Beverly Hills fields, all near the tar pits. "There's no reason to think there's not oil all through there, that they're not connected in some way. That's what the geology tells us." Reinhard was nodding in agreement. "But the real-estate values are too high. Maybe when oil gets to be four hundred dollars a barrel it'd be worth going after, but right now, residential development yields more than oil exploration. Besides, all the mineral rights are tied up, mostly with the original owners of the properties or their heirs.

"In the sixties, when there was that last spate of drilling, if one company would think it had found something to drill, it'd send out teams of leasing agents on Saturday mornings to knock on people's doors, hoping to lock up maybe 50 or 60 percent of the leases before another company caught on by Monday morning.

"You can go in and buy property, but the surface rights to what was underneath were severed long ago. We can't buy those rights, so we pay royalties, anywhere from an eighth to a quarter of every dollar we make. Even for people living in Beverly Hills, that can amount to something significant, especially with prices as high as they are now."

Hearing this triggered another layer of memories and asso-
ciations. I recalled that the Getty house in Hancock Park was a
property that now belonged officially to the office of the mayor
of Los Angeles. Current mayors seem to prefer the greater
privacy of their personal residences, and the old Getty house is
often used as a movie location. Presumably, Getty would have
been happier with ongoing oil royalties than with the occasional
fees paid by the studios when their scouts prospected his house
for a movie location. Driving past my great-grandmother's
house now meant negotiating a street not littered with drilling paraphernalia, but with thick, black cables running from
the backs of semitrailers, where generators were burning that
refined state of oil known as gasoline to power the lights and
cameras.

"What happens to the oil after you bring it up?" I asked. "Do
you ship it or have anything to do with the refining?" Both guys
were shaking their heads.

"Once it's out of the ground, it goes into a pipeline; we don't
know where it goes or who even owns the pipeline. It could
go into one owned by Exxon, be sent to Wilmington or El
Segundo to be refined, and come out as Shell gas at the pump.
For us, we put a molecule in and get paid for it. We're what's
called the upstream part of the industry. You wouldn't believe
how many millions of miles of gas and natural oil pipelines are
out there."

The interview concluding, Washburn carried the Salt Lake
Field photo back to what passed in their offices for a lobby,
really just a space between the front door and the first cubicle
divider. Compulsive counter that I am, I sat on the floor with
the photo and tallied up the derricks, some of which were
hard to distinguish from the evergreens of a windbreak. The

otherwise bare and flat fields of what within a few years would be Park La Brea, the county's recreational Hancock Park and museums, residential Hancock Park, and the street where my great-grandmother lived across from Getty were covered with derricks: 176 by my best count out of three tries.

The idea of burning something other than wood to light the dark dates back more than seventy thousand years, when rocks hollowed out to hold moss soaked in animal fat were used as lamps in the Neolithic Middle East. Until the eighteenth century, the primary fuels used for lighting were whale and fish oil, olive oil and tallow, and beeswax. Not until 1859, when the first well was drilled in Europe for petroleum, did kerosene become a popular alternative, later to be replaced by the safer natural gas, which could be transported citywide through pipes. Gas lighting was replaced when Thomas Edison created the incandescent lightbulb and then went on to do pioneering work on generators that made possible the distribution of electricity. When George Westinghouse insisted that alternating current be used for transmission instead of direct current, despite the higher and more dangerous voltage involved, it became possible to push enough electricity through wires to light entire cities and, eventually, countries. Natural gas was relegated to the kitchen.

In the meantime, however, the automobile was invented, which for many reasons is why Los Angeles spread out the way it did. When Doheny discovered oil downtown in 1892, the city existed in a golden age of preindustrialization. The total population of the county was just over 100,000, and the town had only seventy-eight miles of paved streets. Five years later, the first automobile arrived, a locally built "motor wagon."

Los Angeles County by 1915 had fifty-five thousand privately owned vehicles driving on its streets, which made it the most auto-intensive city in the nation. Five years later, six hundred thousand cars were registered to the county's population of 936,455.

The development of the really large oil fields in the L.A. Basin during the 1920s occurred just as the population of the county doubled—due in large part to the influx of petroleum industry workers and associated businesses. The oil fields themselves were scattered up and down the fault zones, creating the need for transportation of workers and goods. Southern Californians had also already discovered that the automobile was a logical recreational tool enabling them to take advantage of the good weather. The result was the construction of decent roads, which took them to far-flung places with high scenic value.

In 1928 there was a car for every 2.9 persons in the city, most of whom commuted to work, a pattern soon to spread nationwide with the development of suburbs. All this growth was driving up the demand for oil and gasoline and furthering the booming economy of L.A. This in turn attracted more people, who therefore had to drive farther to work, and thus used more gas . . . The area was expanding in an upward spiral of consumption, growth, and demand that hasn't yet ended. Today there are more than fifty-three thousand streets in the city and county. The longest, Sepulveda Boulevard, is seventy-six miles long.

Every city has a metaphorical geography that determines and reflects the nature of its growth. In Los Angeles, petroleum is a widespread fact of nature underfoot, one of the primary reasons for the city to exist, and the fuel that both allowed and necessitated the creation of a grid large enough to cover the basin, therefore determining the warp and weft of its urban fabric.

Ironically, during the latter half of the twentieth century, as we assiduously cultivated environmental awareness, we mostly lost sight of oil in L.A. The energy companies, quite understandably, did everything they could to camouflage their activities, reacting to our growing disdain for visible signs of industrial activity. Derricks were dismantled or covered up to resemble buildings—like the BreitBurn rig on Pico and Genesee avenues, which is camouflaged as an office building—and landscaping was installed around pumps to screen them from view. Only in a few instances are we reminded that what we're walking around on is not a two-dimensional sheet of paper—like the street map we carry in the car—but a planet with three dimensions in space and great depth in time.

Back to the La Brea Tar Pits. The first thing we should do is rid ourselves of the notion that we're dealing with tar, which is a by-product of materials that have a woody origin, such as coal or peat, even though *brea* in Spanish means "tar." This stuff is asphaltum, more commonly called asphalt, which is basically the lowest grade of crude oil and not to be confused with what we drive on, which is pavement, a mixture of asphalt and crushed rock or aggregate. What we call tar pits occur when oil seeps to the surface and the lighter compounds evaporate. What's left is asphalt, which was used for thousand of years by the local Chumash and Gabrielino Indians to caulk baskets and canoes, haft their weapons, and glue together wounds.

The oldest historical known use of asphalt was as a caulking agent in the brick walls of a third millennium BC reservoir in what is now Pakistan. Commercial asphalt was first mined in large quantities from Pitch Lake on the island of Trinidad and is still a major export for use in road construction, though more commonly worldwide, asphalt is now made straight from petroleum. During the 1700s, residents of the pueblo near the La Brea Tar Pits used the asphalt to waterproof their roofs, and under the terms of the 1828 Rancho La Brea land grant, residents were guaranteed access to all the material that they could carry away. Asphalt from the quarry that is now the tar pit was sold by the Hancocks in the 1800s for thirteen to sixteen dollars a ton and was used as far away as San Francisco.

Nowadays, the "tar" is more of a nuisance than anything else in the neighborhood. In the twenty-three acres of Hancock Park, which includes the George C. Page Museum and the Los Angeles County Museum of Art (LACMA), the stuff oozes up inexorably in seeps small and large, a visible reminder that there is indeed an underground geology to Los Angeles. Presumably, that's why the moviemakers chose it as a spot where a volcano pops out of the ground. Angelenos and tourists already accept the area as an active geological site, and audiences would have less disbelief to suspend than if another location had been used.

The park was extensively landscaped in 1998, and the old seeps in the parking lot, for example, were paved over, a peculiar notion perhaps thought of by the county engineers as akin to fighting fire with fire. It didn't work. Where two seeps covering several square yards in the northeast corner parking lot had been blocked off for years with curbing and chain-link fence, workers removed the barriers and laid down fresh pavement. Asphalt and gravel, basically. In roughly the same spots two years later, the pavement was buckled by seeps about six inches in diameter. Every couple of seconds, a bubble of natural gas one-half inch across burbled up to the surface. Maintenance crews spread kitty litter around the two sticky spots, but there were always black tire and dog tracks leading off in several directions.

Then there are the seeps in the grass. These are more insidious in that, should you step on a small seep not barricaded off, though you won't sink to an ignominious depth and have to be rescued by the fire department—as you would if you were mucking about in the tar pits—you will carry away with you one of nature's more tenacious substances. The slight sucking sound your shoes will make as you walk across a linoleum floor leaving behind tiny black bits for your mate to step on and, in turn, to disperse farther through the house is the sound of domestic doom. I've often wondered why Tommy Lee Jones and Anne Heche didn't have to cope with this facet of the Park La Brea disaster in *Volcano*.

Petroleum, its by-products, and associated elements are virtually omnipresent across the Los Angeles Basin, which was obvious from even a glance at the map hanging on Hal Washburn's office. The state's oil and gas division does have a standing policy that opposes construction on top of old oil wells, but that hasn't prevented a developer from expanding the historical Farmers Market with a contemporary addition, "The Grove," which features upscale national-chain retail stores and movie theaters abutting BreitBurn's Salt Lake Field facility. It's a matter of opinion whether this proximity should make anyone nervous. The construction of a subway tunnel was the fictional pretext leading to the eruption of the La Brea Tar Pits, but those of us who lived in the neighborhood pretty much shrugged our shoulders at the expansion of the marketplace.

Natural gas, composed mostly of methane and ethane, is extremely flammable when not dispersed, a fact that must have astonished the people living in Iran when they first discovered natural gas seeps sometime between 6000 and 2000 BC. In fact, a common theory about why ancient Persians worshiped fire is that a lightning strike ignited one of the seeps. At several points along my street in Park La Brea, tall, white plastic pipes rose from the ground, climbed up the two-story townhouses, and vented wild methane away from kitchen windows—a clever contradiction in that we use tame, that is, metered, natural gas in our stoves. During thunderstorms, which are rare enough in L.A. to warrant watching, I had the habit of standing at the front door and watching through the screen as bolts hit the E! Entertainment tower. Only as I was writing this paragraph did it occur to me that this could have made for a more exciting and religious event than I was prepared to witness, had lightning somehow managed to ignite a pocket of methane in the neighborhood.

The Chinese first mentioned natural gas as a useful resource some three thousand years ago, and by 211 BC, they were drilling wells for it as deep as five hundred feet by driving bamboo poles into the ground. The gas wasn't known as a source of energy in Europe until 1659, and not used in the United States until 1821, when gas from a well in Fredonia, New York, was piped to homes for light fixtures and stoves.

Methane is not something you want to spend much time breathing. Apart from its extreme flammability, it's not rated by the Environmental Protection Agency (EPA) as a particularly hazardous toxin. But when combined with steam, methane yields carbon monoxide and, in sufficient concentrations, can suffocate you. Methane's toxicity is relatively benign, however, when compared with the hydrogen sulfide that often accompanies natural gas. Also a product of organic decomposition, this sulfurous compound gives off the classic rotten-egg odor we associate with swamps, marshes, and the northwest corner of the county's Hancock Park. If the stoplight at the intersection of Fairfax and Sixth streets is red, the odor accumulates quickly enough in the car to make you roll up the windows and put the fan on recirculation mode.

Methane under certain conditions can burn so hot and clean that it's invisible; you literally can't see the flame and can just blunder into it. In a corollary fashion, hydrogen sulfide, when it occurs at concentrations of 3–5 parts per million (ppm), is only a nasty smell; at 100 ppm, however, it deadens your olfactory sense, which means you no longer know you're in danger. Exposure to this gas over several minutes in the 250-ppm range renders you unconscious; at 1,000 ppm, you need only take one or two breaths of the gas before it kills you.

Hydrogen sulfide, which occurs naturally around oil fields, is a leading cause of death in the workplace, according to the EPA's Web site. Chronic exposure in low amounts over long periods can cause cognitive disorders such as memory and speech impairment in humans; experiments with animals suggest that a loss of tissue mass may also occur if the gas is encountered chronically during the development of the brain. Tests to determine if long-term exposure is carcinogenic have never been run, and it's no wonder that the Los Angeles Unified School District is continually nervous about the schools it has built over old oil fields. The known wells are capped, but no one knows how securely, and the associated gases tend to migrate around human barriers.

Another reminder that Angelenos live on top of oil was in fact one of the more controversial and visible collisions of nature and culture in the basin. The controversy involved the construction of the Belmont Learning Complex near downtown and

atop the Los Angeles City Oil Field, not very far from the site
of Doheny's discovery. In 1999, members of the school board
halted work in midconstruction on the $200 million facility, the
nation's most expensive high school, when both methane and
hydrogen sulfide were detected. The oil field, which lies only six
hundred feet beneath the surface, extends west from Alameda
Street in downtown to Vermont Avenue in Hollywood over
a four-mile stretch and was drilled mostly before 1915. At its
height, it contained 1,200 to 1,500 wells, most of which have
long since been abandoned and are virtually invisible, though
roughly 300 are unaccounted for. Only 6 to 8 old wells remain
on the new school site, most of them already capped. Thomas
Gold might have noted with approval that the field appears
to be repressurizing with oil and water. The repressurization
increases a hazard already complicated by the lack of knowledge about the exact location of all the wells on the property.

One of the construction project directors, Edwin Weyrauch,
pointed out that the site was typical of the L.A. Basin. In fact,
the entire coast of California is riddled with fissures leaking
petroleum-related substances to the surface. You can walk along
beds of hardened asphaltum on the shores near Santa Barbara
and beachcomb for tar balls formed by undersea seepages and
washed ashore. In November 1999, a retired oil engineer took
a *Los Angeles Times* reporter on a walk around the area and
pointed out leaking wells and pipes, wondering why, if the new
Belmont site was so dangerous, the city was allowing construction of new apartment complexes nearby. The original Belmont
High School, in fact, sits directly atop abandoned wells on the
field, as do eight other schools and three hospitals in the county,
all of them exposed to the same hazards as those affecting the
half-completed complex.

Weyrauch was fighting a losing battle against the evolution of human cognition. What we do in L.A. is what we do when living in any environment that is visibly large and complex. We simplify it, a process natural to our neurological makeup. Of all the information we take in, 80 percent is visual—a hundred million bits per second stream in through our eyes, a flow our brain ruthlessly pares down to a trickle, lest it be overcome with data and crash. At a higher level of cognition, we do something similar when living in a congested environment: We automatically edit out information in order to go about the business of living. We become accustomed to certain sights, and even hazards, which surface in our consciousness only when noticing them is necessary. We say that a problem "comes to light," meaning it becomes visible, only when it potentially or immediately intrudes on our functioning, an evolutionary trait left over from when a problem meant a threat to survival, not merely an inconvenience.

I became aware of this kind of cognitive shunting almost every time I drove from Park La Brea to the Los Angeles International Airport (LAX) to pick up a first-time visitor to the city. I would usually take La Cienega Boulevard through the Baldwin Hills, the only city street I know of in America where traffic routinely exceeds sixty-five miles per hour. Concentrating on traffic going up and over the short pass heading southward, I wouldn't pay much attention to the Inglewood Oil Field that I was traversing, the most visible field in the city. But on the return trip with my passengers, their exclamations would remind me of what we were seeing: There are few cities in the world where the road from the airport passes through a working oil field.

I usually tried to count how many wells were pumping, to

determine whether the field was getting more active or less. Then I would estimate how many rigs I could actually see drilling new wells within sight. On average, I found at least two. After meeting with Hal Washburn and Reinhard Suchland at BreitBurn, I could at least envision the fault that runs underneath the hills and allows the oil to be tapped. And just as the unusual orientation of my street kept the La Brea Tar Pits in my mind, so La Cienega Boulevard provided a reminder of the larger geological reality underlying the basin. Being reminded of the uniqueness by someone to whom the sight is new at first flipped me into a more multidimensional consideration of the space around me. After I began work on this book, the fourth dimension of time intruded more and more on my perceptions.

Los Angeles is one of the most scrutinized cities in the world, certainly through film, but also through books, the two information cultures actually going hand in hand more easily than you might think. L.A. is not only the film capital of the world, but also the largest book market in America. And both the book and the film industries depend on writers to keep them going. This makes for a large number of resident writers, no matter that they're dispersed over the metro area's 465 square miles. Among that population is Mike Davis, author of a left-leaning cultural and urban planning analysis of Los Angeles, *City of Quartz*, which received almost universal acclaim. He followed it up with another book that was not so well received.

Ecology of Fear resembles *City of Quartz* in that it relies on reams of research into facts that most people have purged from the forefront of their awareness. Starting with the inescapable geographical facts of Los Angeles—that it is prone to

earthquakes, floods, mudslides, brushfires, and even modest
tornadoes, which tend to head for LAX—Davis notes how
books and movies alike dwell on apocalyptic scenarios for the
city, the exact subgenre into which *Volcano* fit. As literary critics have also noted, the imaginations of L.A. writers insist on
canceling out the Chamber of Commerce's equating the place
with a Mediterranean paradise. For example, television weather
forecasters follow the party line of developers and often dismiss
the local tornadoes as "freak winds"; meanwhile, writers such
as Steve Erickson envision terminal floods for the basin.

Some of us relished Davis's revisionist history of Los Angeles,
which analyzed the intertwined ecological and social dystopia
sitting underneath the cheerful boosterism of the local real-
estate industry, the leaders of which would prefer to ignore
the city's penchant for natural disasters. But the business community reacted with fury to what it considered his unnecessary
trashing of the city's reputation. These are people who will fight
to keep L.A. as a location for filming disaster flicks because
movie productions are good for the local economy—and as
long as the earthquakes or floods or tsunamis, as in the movie
Escape from L.A., are fictional. Discuss such disasters in terms
of factual probabilities, however, and you become a threat.

Of course, we all love a good disaster at a distance, and what
appears to be a local obsession with apocalyptic upheavals of
nature has one of its roots in eighteenth-century European
culture, which began to present volcanoes, for instance, to the
public as entertainment in the form of paintings. Tiring of the
merely picturesque landscapes that were the fashion, English
artists traveled the world in search of stronger stuff. Using their
topographical schooling to accurately depict the sublime features of the earth, from Antarctic icebergs to Alpine glaciers,

these itinerant artists were important agents in broadening
scientific observation during the great era of exploration, as
well as precursors to the romantics who would follow them in
the next century.

A good example is Joseph Wright of Derby. A classically
trained English landscape painter, Wright journeyed to Italy in
the 1770s and painted the eruption of Vesuvius. His paintings
were the only accurate pictorial representation most people in
England were likely to see of volcanic activity until the inven-
tion of the camera. One of his Vesuvius oil paintings hangs at
the Huntington Library in Pasadena, a large canvas cast largely
in reds and oranges reflecting the lava pouring down the slopes.
The picture is popular with visitors and one that I visit frequently, both to admire its place in the natural history of images
and simply for the visceral thrill it offers.

The American painter Frederic Church, working almost
a century later, executed enormous canvases representing in
great detail the geography and ecosystems of foreign places.
Inspired by his mentor, the explorer and naturalist Alexander
von Humboldt, Church voyaged twice to South America. On
his second trip, a return to Ecuador, he was able to paint the
impressive volcano Cotopaxi, which was in almost constant
eruption while he was there. Church's exhibitions of his panoramic views of climactic scenery, from Niagara Falls to the
Andes, were vastly popular in London and New York. Thousands of people flocked to see the paintings, which were often
displayed singly as if feature attractions in a movie theater. The
visitors paid an entrance fee and, in some cases, received opera
glasses through which to view the scenery, which was framed
by live plants imported from the countryside depicted. His 1862
oil painting *Cotopaxi*, which resides in the Detroit Institute of

Art, shows the volcano spewing a column of ash that the wind has blown in front of the sun, turning the entire world into a vision straight out of Dante. In the foreground a waterfall cascades into a rugged gorge, and the whole effect is as dramatic as the lava pouring down Wilshire, which is the real star of the movie *Volcano*.

Ecology of Fear proposed that we have insisted on building a city in the known path of multiple natural disasters and that a theme park of the apocalypse would be more appropriate to symbolize the region than the pastel fantasies of Disneyland. Perhaps Davis is right. Perhaps this relentless fictional destruction of L.A. is a paranoid reaction to the inescapable environmental dangers behind the city's facade of surf and sun. On the other hand, maybe Angelenos like disaster movies simply because the films show that humans can survive earthquakes, fire, and floods. Either way, the fictions are a counterbalance to our fears.

A more mundane explanation for the recurring theme may coexist alongside such theories. L.A. is where most of the world's big-budget movies are made. From several centuries of a visual culture that presented them with such spectacles, American audiences have been trained to expect and even demand staged natural disasters. It's usually cheaper to set the disasters in L.A., no matter how improbable, than to go on location elsewhere. (As a side note, eleven weeks before *Volcano* came out, another molten extravaganza was released. *Dante's Peak*, starring Pierce Brosnan, was filmed in the Pacific Northwest and cost $15 million more to make.)

The critics of *Ecology of Fear* had nothing to fear from the book. It didn't scare off prospective visitors or residents, and L.A. remains one of the fastest-growing metro areas in the country. To be sure, Davis knows a useful hyperbole when he sees one, but even his long list of possible disasters was far from complete. Other than mentioning what might happen to the coastal oil refineries should they explode as the result of an earthquake, he didn't even touch what it means to continue to expand one of the largest cities in the world on top of one of its largest and densest petroleum basins.

No matter why we destroy L.A. so frequently in our imaginations, when a hazard reaches a high enough perceptual level that it becomes a media event, as in the case of the Belmont Learning Center, we trust the sometimes illogical nature of our perceptions. That is, if we didn't pay attention to it before, it wasn't important enough to worry about. If we're paying attention now, then the threat must be real. After all, we've trusted our cognitive triage for millions of years to keep us out of danger, and for the most part, it has worked.

Once the Belmont scare had enough of a run on television and in the newspapers, not to mention the radio talk shows, most people tended to cross off the site mentally as a viable one, despite the assurances of engineers that stray gas could be collected into pipes and burned harmlessly. Maybe it was the fact that in 1985—the same year that the basement of the Ross store blew up—a methane vent opened up in the middle of Fairfax Street and burned uncontrollably for days before it could be put out. The event was remembered by some of my neighbors with relish and made people there just a tiny bit skeptical. Or that, in March 1962, a Hawthorne woman had a fire under her house—a house with no basement. She located the source of the problem when she went outside and touched a match to a crack in the sidewalk: A flame ran down it.

If walking over to the tar pits and watching the methane bubbles didn't refocus me when I needed a break from the computer keyboard, I would go look at the saber-toothed cats. Or, to be precise, their skulls, one hundred of them lined up in long rows along a long backlit wall in the Page Museum, one of the more startling natural-history installations in America.

Most people who noticed the bones in the tar pits during the nineteenth century assumed they belonged to cattle that had wandered out onto the asphalt, perhaps seeking a drink of water from the shallow pond that sometimes covered the pits. Especially during the spring and summer months, heat softens the goo to a treacherous degree. In 1875, amateur paleontologists uncovered prehistoric bones, but it wasn't until 1901 that John C. Merriam, a professor from the University of California at Berkeley, arrived to make the first scientific excavations. By 1915, exclusive rights to excavate had been granted to the Natural History Museum of Los Angeles County, and the next year, Hancock donated 23 of his 4,400 acres to the county for the park.

According to the Page Museum, since 1906, a million-plus bones have been recovered from more than one hundred excavation sites around the tar pits. The museum now has on hand the remains of more than two thousand individual saber-toothed cats, along with those of other charismatic ice age megafauna, such as mammoths, mastodons, dire wolves, and the gigantic short-faced bear. For thirty thousand years, 231 species of unwary vertebrates were trapped in the soft asphaltum that lay just beneath a shallow layer of water. Thirty thousand doesn't sound like a large number of years compared with the five- to ten-million-year-old oil underneath the pits, but consider this: If only ten animals were snared every thirty years, that would easily account for the fossils from all the ten thousand individual animals that have been recovered.

Eight to twelve gallons of asphalt still ooze up in the tar pits every day. Lizards, pigeons, assorted rodents, sometimes a hawk or an egret, and even dogs and people still manage to invade the fence and get stuck. Only one human skeleton has ever been found in the excavations, that of a woman resembling a Chumash Indian from approximately nine thousand years ago. Forensics revealed that she had suffered a violent blow to the head; theories about how and why the victim of L.A.'s first noir mystery ended up in the pit are manifold and inconclusive.

The La Brea Tar Pits are fenced off and patrolled, the gases vented carefully away from people and structures, and except for visitors who get asphaltum on the soles of their shoes, the hazards of the area seem to have been mitigated. When I visit the museums, I always find bubbling up under the lawn new seeps, around which little exclosures of wooden stakes have been strung with yellow plastic tape upon which is printed endlessly "Caution: Do Not Enter." One part of the park or another always looks like a crime scene. According to the maintenance crews I queried, seventeen sumps are scattered around the property, and every two to three months, trucks arrive to pump out the "tar."

Every year, Park La Brea and the other apartment buildings in the area likewise pump out the mixture of petroleum and water that seeps into lawns, basements, and underground parking garages. The water is separated from the asphaltum and sent down the storm drains; the residue, for which the city will assume no responsibility, is hauled away by semitrailer rigs bearing special containers owned by private companies that specialize in handling solid waste. The private operators charge up to three hundred dollars a barrel to remove it; then they refine and sell what's left as a low-grade petroleum product.

BreitBurn's Salt Lake Field operation, as well as other wells throughout the basin, is inspected on a regular basis by the state's Department of Conservation. Gas detectors, frequent equipment checks, and fire suppression equipment are all in place. That doesn't change the fact that the earth beneath your feet there moves in violent and unpredictable ways more often than most other places in the country. Nor does it make fissures leaking methane and hydrogen sulfide desirable features on Fairfax Avenue, much less in a high school basement. Nor does it minimize the danger from the uncounted miles of aging pipelines running beneath the city. In Long Beach in 1994, for instance, twenty-four thousand barrels of petroleum-contaminated water leaked into the Los Angeles River, necessitating the replacement of more than twenty miles of pipe. More recent spills have drained out into, and helped pollute, the coastal waters.

Nature and our engineering of it are dangerous to one degree or another, everywhere, all the time, but the hazards to Los Angeles have been lived with for well over a century. It's continually important to sort out the difference between movies about volcanoes, no matter how good the special effects in your neighborhood, and, say, the more subtle realities of the Sixth Street Fault, which is named after the street I crossed to reach the tar pits. It's not that I was fond of living in Los Angeles, but the tar pits revealed and placed in the foreground of my thinking a four-dimensional nature that would otherwise be more obscured. I welcomed the occasional smell of rotten eggs drifting up from the kitchen sink, even while I was holding my breath.

The smell of hydrogen sulfide and the ruminations over the

tar pits led me to an awareness of not just the present tense of
surface asphalt, but of the depth of the ground beneath my feet
and the depth of our ignorance. I'd initially gone over to the tar
pits to stretch my legs and uncrinkle my mind, visiting a local
tourist spot to get away from the essay on my desk; I returned
with an entirely new set of concerns.

For example, what does it mean to displace tons of water
in the L.A. Basin every day to mine oil and gas, a practice that
changes the way earthquakes react with the ground on which
we build? And what does it mean to bring forth an energy
resource buried in the past, in deep time, and use it now, an
activity that seriously alters the heat balance of the planet?
If you prematurely excavate resources that natural processes
would otherwise recirculate over millions, even billions, of
years in the tectonic churning of the earth's crust, and if you use
them all at once, can the planetary surface handle the outpour-
ing of chemicals and heat? And what resources are left for the
future—not the near future of our children and grandchildren,
but, say, the third millennium AD?

I wondered, too, about the human cognitive conditions
underlying these questions. For instance, can we train ourselves
to use a sensory memory, such as smell, to short-circuit the
cognitive processes that allow us to conveniently forget threats
that are not immediate? Humans recognize approximately ten
thousand smells; the sandstone core I'd held in my hand in the
BreitBurn offices had immediately taken me back to dragging
Virginia Street in Reno in 1967. Our sense of smell is directly
linked to our limbic system, the 45-million-year-old neural net
in the brain that governs our emotions and motivations, an evolutionary survival tool that is intimately tied to how we learn
and remember. Sensory impressions and experiences can be

stored in the limbic system for up to three years before they're either deleted or made long-term memories. What experience was going to have a better chance of becoming something I'd not forget in three years—the smell of the sandstone core, or watching the movie *Volcano*?

It occurred to me that time had something to do with this: not only the dredging up of resources from the far left-hand side of the timeline, the geological epochs and evolution of human cognition, but even our near-term memory. With the median age at Park La Brea sinking down to thirty-two from what used to be its status in the 1980s as a retirement community, the memories of the Ross store's basement blowing up were fading rapidly out of the culture.

We experience time in two ways: sequence and duration. Sequence comes unbidden to us; a sensory impression is formed, then another, then another. We also have minds that are hierarchical, that automatically rank information from less to more important. Creating layers of sequences, whether in a movie or in geological strata, is an aggregating ability wired genetically into our brains. How we perceive duration invokes the use of another cognitive ability, memory. The mind is able to perceive directly a stimulus lasting only about two seconds before it must invoke memory to sustain recognition of the event.

The links between memory and cognition, between place and our effects on it, and how we treat place in popular culture, especially in Los Angeles, were going to take some investigating. For one thing, as Alison Hawthorne Deming points out in *The Monarchs,* her extended poem sequence on the natural navigation of butterflies and the human heart, time itself is what allows us to perceive the world. She relates the story of an experimental psychologist who, projecting a picture onto a device mounted

to his subject's eye, moved the image at the same speed at which
the woman's eye tracked it, thus making it invisible to her. Only
when the image was still or moved at a speed out of coordina-
tion with the tiny sweeping motions made by the eyes could
she identify the object projected in front of her. To paraphrase
Gregory Bateson, the anthropologist: "All information is news
of difference." And time is what creates difference.

It's by being out of synch with the ongoing present, or what
we refer to as "real time," through experiencing the past and
imagining the future, that we're able to perceive where we are,
what our place is. Even if we maintain a sense of sequence,
without being able to judge duration or invoke memory, we
lose our place in the sequence.

The problem is not just that people don't have time to tell
stories to one another or that generations increasingly are isolated from one another, so that the memory of the Ross basement's blowing up is conveniently misplaced as a hazard we can
ignore. It's also that almost everyone, except for the kids in the
LACMA parking lot, walks too fast to notice the tar oozing up
through the asphalt or, seeing it, fails to consider what it means.
And it's also a result of how media fold time in front of us. If the
Wilshire Boulevard in *Volcano* was re-created at seven-eighths
scale, space manipulated to fit the budget and the focal length of
the lenses, that's nothing compared with Hollywood's compression of time. On celluloid, events over two days are squeezed
into 103 minutes, and the lava—the fictional apocalyptic geology of the basin—is channeled out to sea in a paved creek bed
to save the Beverly Center from being consumed.

Many Hollywood movies do everything they can to match
the speed of their images to our attention spans, reinforcing a
trend toward more but shorter experiences of greater intensity,

a temporal synergy that threatens to erase the world in front of us as surely as experimental psychologists did with their subjects. It's a method of subsuming the past and future into an endless sense of the present, which asserts that we can solve any conflict within two hours, three tops, up to and including massive fountains of magma at the end of your street.

A TOUR OF THE ANTENNAE

The landscape had gone all lunar, blackened earth dotted here and there with the charred skeletal remains of chamise and scrub oak trees creaking in a thirty-mile-per-hour Santa Ana wind. Gusts were strong enough to make me stagger slightly as I followed the Temescal Ridge Trail one blustery March day to the top of Green Mountain, a prominent knoll in the Santa Monica Mountains that rises between Topanga Canyon to the west and Sunset Boulevard to the southeast. The only things green about the mountain, where the fire had burned around all four sides at the top, were a few clumps of grass and weeds reestablishing themselves after the sparse winter rains.

On top of Green Mountain sat a modest artifactual site, a concrete block building that anchored a forty-foot-tall telecommunications mast hosting five short antennae. The building was caged in a square of rusty chain-link fence, out of which the mast protruded skyward. Double guy wires anchored the mast in four directions, and a black power cable ran from the nearby power poles and into the assemblage. Two more antennae were mounted to corners of the wire exclosure, around the top of which were strung a half dozen strands of sagging barbed wire.

I'd been walking in the wind for two hours, enjoying the views of Mount San Antonio (aka Mount Baldy) in the San Gabriels to the northeast, the Santa Ynez range to the east of Santa Barbara, and then down south to the Palos Verdes Peninsula and out to Catalina Island. But I was also ready for a break and glad to sit in the lee of the small building to eat my lunch. It took a few minutes to catch my breath, settle my heartbeat, and change my visual processing from walking to sitting, from being an object in motion through the landscape to a stationary being in the middle of what turned out to be a landscape in motion.

Following the power lines along the ridge, I'd been accompanied by a concert of moaning, whistling, keening, and what sounded like the faint whine of commercial jet aircraft flying overhead. All these sounds were caused by the wind and vibrating wires. When sitting, I could see that the burned trees were waving, that dirt was flowing in short eddies across the ground, and that even the heavily braced double power poles were rocking in the wind. I stood up and pushed my way over to one of the guys, placing my fingertips on it. It didn't appear to be moving, but I could feel it tremble, a cycle of vibration so fast it was a tactile blur.

While I was up, I made a circuit around the site in between the gusts, attempting to take notes about what I could see inside the chain-link fence. Within a minute, I gave up trying to write and concentrated instead on just observing until I passed back into the lee. Returning to where I'd left my pack, I sat again to scribble down what I'd seen: rusty wire, a faded Coca-Cola can, stiffened fragments of duct tape, a broom with an orange handle, one empty water bottle, and a new collinear antenna lying inside its box on the ground, a seventy-six-pound item addressed to Green Mountain. And one lizard clinging precariously to the side of the building, watching me as I wrote.

Outside the cage were two bronze triangulation disks mounted into concrete blocks and set flush with the ground. Placed in 1950, according to their incised dates, they were first-order survey control points set down by the Los Angeles Department of Public Works, just two of the thousands of physical reference points around the basin. The points align the local civic infrastructure to the largest rectilinear grid on the planet, the national survey designed by Thomas Jefferson in the 1780s. In turn, the national grid is set within the great cartographic graticule that has been painstakingly wrapped around the planet since the ancient Greeks. The modest disks anchor us in space by virtue of the survey, but also in time, acknowledging the particular colonization of the United States within a global history. Overlooking the Pacific Ocean, the survey points exist on the terminus of our cartographic imperative, where our American idea of Manifest Destiny drove our population during the mid-nineteenth century.

From atop the ridge, I could see areas of brown turbidity in the ocean, the wind kicking up waves that in turn were lifting sand off the bottom. The surface of everything I could see was either moving in front of my eyes or showed evidence of that motion, whether it was from the Santa Anas or the winds of history. But what about invisible motion? I thought to myself. What about the waves in the air—waves that I couldn't see and that were being propagated across the L.A. Basin by the antenna standing behind me?

The antenna was invented by German physicist Heinrich Hertz, who in the late 1880s was attempting to verify James Clerk Maxwell's 1864 mathematical proof that an entire spectrum of electromagnetic energy, of which visible light was only a small portion, was passing through the air. Hertz set up sparking devices between two parabolic mirrors facing each other and about five feet apart. When he sent an electrical current into one device, causing a short arc, the other also sparked, thus verifying in experiment what Maxwell's mathematics had proposed. Shortly thereafter the Italian physicist Guglielmo Marconi repeated the experiment, increasing the distance to thirty feet. By 1901 he was sending point-to-point wireless electromagnetic signals—radio waves—across the Atlantic, from Cornwall to Newfoundland. Wireless telegraphy was routinely being used between shore and ships in 1910, the year when signals were also first successfully exchanged between land and airplanes.

American Telephone & Telegraph managed to transmit speech by radio from Arlington, Virginia, to Paris in 1915, the same year that advertisements were first sent not just point to point, but cast broadly to anyone listening in. With the financial incentive of a mass audience, radio operators began an encirclement of the globe that would make the mapping grid with its 16.6 billion intersecting points of the degrees, minutes, and seconds of latitude and longitude look insignificant. The boom had to wait until after World War I, because during the war, the private use of radio was restricted for tactical purposes. By 1920, however, the country's first commercial radio station went on the air from Pittsburgh. Money spent on the purchase of radios, as the engineer Henry Petroski notes in his book *Remaking the World,* grew from $60 million in 1922 to more than $350 million two years later.

Television, the electromagnetic broadcasting of images along with sound, was invented in the 1930s and, after World War II, quickly became ubiquitous in American households. Just as World War I had prompted vast improvements in radio technology, so did World War II produce advances in electronics that made television viable as a commercial telecommunications medium. By the time I was a kid growing up in San Diego during the 1950s, the roof of almost every house I saw had an antenna, a straight metal pole with a directional array pointed at the nearest broadcasting tower.

A century after Marconi first sent radio signals across the Atlantic, the fastest-growing telecommunications network was PCS—personal communications services, otherwise known as wireless voice, fax, and data transmission—a return to wireless point-to-point usage. In 1997 alone, Sprint PCS, just one company among many, erected fifty thousand new cell-phone towers. Fifteen hundred other companies had received PCS licenses in the United States and were erecting antennae on everything in sight: churches, billboards, water tanks, office and apartment buildings, highway signs. In fact, along some interstate freeways, such as the relatively scenic I-25 between Albuquerque and Santa Fe, the distinction of being the most intrusive vertical features had by mid-decade already become a contest between billboards and cell-phone towers. In Los Angeles, although oil derricks often were disguised as miniature office buildings, telecommunication towers on the ridgetops, built along the same design lines, stood as bold icons of their industry.

After writing about the La Brea Tar Pits, I became increasingly aware that my subject was more than just the visible conjunctions of nature and culture, or land and landscape, but also the invisible ones surrounding us. We can't see most of the electromagnetic spectrum that's now flowing around and through us any more than we can view the wind. It's only what generates the wind and the signals, and what the two carry along on waves of varying amplitude, that we can perceive. We can watch the sunlight falling on the ocean, for instance, which then changes the temperature and creates pressure differentials from which winds are born. And we can visit the transmitters and antennae that send and receive the radio, television, and PCS signals.

The historical mother lode of all antennae infestations in the Los Angeles area is located on the steep ridges of Mount Wilson, a peak that looms over Pasadena. Unlike on Green Mountain, where the wind was playing an aeolian harp, on Mount Wilson, at six thousand feet in the San Gabriels, the Santa Ana winds boom in a forest of steel towers so thick you feel as if you'd stumbled into the interior of a pipe organ. If the La Brea Tar Pits were the visible tip of the nature underground and in deep time, the telecommunication towers and the nearby telescopes represented a struggle between time and instantaneity. It was time to walk back to the car and plan a trip into the San Gabriels.

According to Mike Davis, Los Angeles has the longest wild edge of any nontropical city in the world. Tract homes and shopping malls collide with desert and primarily mountains along a 675-mile-long boundary that, as the metropolitan area constantly expands, grows longer every year. Much of the city's northern edge is defined by the 63-mile-long San Gabriel Mountains, home to populations of deer, coyote, black bear, bighorn sheep, and mountain lions and to stands of chamise, manzanita, Douglas fir, Coulter pine, and cedar. Although the San Gabriels suffer under more than 32 million visitor trips per year, their thousand square miles manage to retain a surprisingly large and healthy biological diversity because the terrain is so steep and because more than 80 percent of its surface is overgrown with impenetrable chaparral. The range has been billed by writers from Davis to John McPhee as, variously, the steepest, fastest-rising, and most precipitously eroding mountains in North America, and I was slowly acquainting myself with them.

For most of my life, I've been fortunate to live within the shadow of multiple mountain ranges: in Reno, the Sierra

Nevada and the Virginias; in Santa Fe, the Sangre de Cristo, Jemez, Ortiz, and Sandias; and in Los Angeles, the Santa Monicas, San Gabriels, and San Bernardinos. As a result, no matter where I've lived, I've been in sight of telecommunication towers. From Reno, it was the radio and television transmitters atop both Peavine and Slide mountains; in Santa Fe it was a collection on Tesuque Peak, at 12,040 feet a popular hiking and cross-country ski objective. The Sandias above Albuquerque, where I often drove to see friends, offered a stunning array of towers and antennae at the end of a long hike up from the valley floor, a collection often covered on winter mornings with brilliant hoarfrost and snow. The only mountains that I can remember that were free of antennae were the Southern Alps of New Zealand and the Nepalese Himalaya. No doubt that's no longer true.

More often than not, even in remote areas, the higher vantage points are surmounted with antennae. In fact, given the military's penchant for solitude in which to practice different versions of apocalypse, or the prevention thereof, the desert peaks of the American West offer a remarkable array of radar domes, portable targeting systems, electronic warfare range facilities, and a shining miscellany of metal towers. From where I lived in L.A., the civilian broadcast tower atop 1,600-foot Mount Lee in Griffith Park, just east of the Hollywood sign, was in view whenever the air was clear. But none of these approached the artificial forest on Mount Wilson.

Communicating from the tops of mountains is hardly a new idea. The word *telegraphy* comes from the Greek *tele*, "distance," and *graphein*, "to write," but *telegraphy* is a term used so broadly that it includes shouting and drumming over long distances, as well as sending electrical signals over wires. Native

Americans used signal fires on the highest peaks of the Great Basin to send messages across the deserts of today's Nevada and Utah. Some of the same peaks were used by the surveyors of the nineteenth and early twentieth centuries as they mapped the region and attempted to measure more accurately the size of the earth. Instead of using fire at night to communicate, they reflected sunlight from the three-inch mirrors of their heliotropes, bouncing beams to each other up to a hundred miles away. Now we use lasers to measure from peak to peak, and global positioning system (GPS) units can measure the elevation of high points by triangulating off multiple satellites even higher above us.

In the seventeenth century, the telescope was being used to extend the ability of people to see messages with flags, and in 1791, the Frenchman Claude Chappe had translated this into the semaphore, two pivoting arms mounted on towers three to six miles apart. The arms could be maneuvered into forty-nine combinations to represent the letters of the alphabets and other shorthand terms. Chappe, using his system to bring to Paris news of a conflict with the Austrians, was accorded the title *telegraph engineer.* In 1795, the Englishman George Murray invented the shutter telegraph, which flashed light signals between elevated sites that were often named Telegraph Hill or Signal Hill. By 1837, the U.S. Congress, frustrated with the slow speed of communication across the nation's rapidly growing territory, was considering the establishment of a national semaphore line when Samuel Morse approached the government for support of his electrical telegraph system.

Morse, a painter who was passionate about the study of electromagnetism, knew that a burst of electricity sent through a wire could ring a bell as far as a mile away. Modifying the current with the help of a key not unlike that found on a piano, he devised dots and dashes—short and long signals—that could be transcribed by a listener. In 1844, he strung a thirty-seven-mile wire from Washington, D.C., to Baltimore, and thus was born the telecommunications industry. One of the scenic climaxes of that industry is found atop Mount Wilson.

Driving up to the 5,712-foot summit from the Los Angeles Basin is to ascend through increasingly colder climate zones, passing each thousand-foot gain in elevation as if going north from latitude to latitude. The desertlike chaparral that resides in between the green lawns of Northridge below gives way to evergreen forest above, and snowbanks still bordered the road at the summit a few weeks after my hike up Green Mountain. It was like driving backward in time a few months to Christmas. I had expected the most visible sign of human occupation at the top of Mount Wilson to be its famous observatory. Instead, I found myself winding around the perimeter of a forest of steel towers that in some places dominated the terrain much more completely than the pine trees.

I parked at an overlook where I could peer out over the basin, but much of the vista was obscured by that almost-perpetual haze known as *air-light,* generated by the collision of airborne dust and marine air. The Santa Ana winds blowing on the mountain had yet to reach the plains below. One of the more prevalent particles in the Los Angeles air is material eroded out of the San Gabriel Mountains. The particles end up as bits of dust approximately one-half micrometer in diameter—the same diameter as the wavelength of light, as Lawrence Weschler pointed out in a *New Yorker* article about the atmospheric qualities of Southern California. The subsequent ubiquitous reflection of sunlight by billions upon billions of those dust particles creates the white haze—as opposed to the yellow or brown pall of smog—that often obscures all but the most immediate local topography.

Another thing about L.A.'s air is that it is relatively stable; warm desert air from high elevations flows down through the passes at the eastern ends of the basin, trapping the denser, colder air below it. This creates inversions that led Spanish sailors, observing the accumulated layer of pollution from Indian campfires hanging over the future site of the city, to call the place the Bay of Smokes—and this was a century before the creation of automobile smog. But at high elevations, the inversions preserve the astonishingly clear desert air. This is a boon for astronomical observations, which is why many of the most significant telescopic discoveries during the first half of the twentieth century were made at the observatories of Southern California.

Turning my back on the view, I strolled along the narrow asphalt roads of the crest until I had left behind the sequoias of the telecommunications industry and entered the more sober compound of the observatories. Mount Wilson has a distinguished history with both mirrors and electromagnetic signals. In 1864, Benjamin Wilson, a mayor of Los Angeles—whose grandson, General George Patton, would have his own use for signals in both world wars—built a burro trail to the top of the mountain in search of lumber for his ranch in the valley below. He soon abandoned his quest and the trail fell into disrepair; apart from the rare hunter or prospector, the mountaintop was seldom visited. John Muir prowled through the area in 1877, noting that it was as inaccessible as any range he had previously attempted to traverse. A year later, he would lead a government survey party to the top of Mount Troy in central south Nevada, where they would establish one of the Great Arc Triangulation heliotrope stations.

While Muir was tramping up and down the peaks of California, the valleys below were filling up with people, and the broad bowl at the foot of what was still known as Wilson's Peak was no exception. In 1873, emigrant families from Indiana had established a community, which two years later would be incorporated as Pasadena. In the 1880s, Wilson's Peak became a popular destination for midwesterners seeking to escape from frigid winters; the trail up the peak was refurbished, and the nine-mile horseback ride, which took two days round-trip, became a popular outing. In 1893, on a peak just four miles west of Mount Wilson, an engineer named Thaddeus Lowe opened a three-thousand-foot-long, narrow-gauge cable line that lifted open-sided railway cars filled with passengers to the summit. Mount Lowe became an even more popular tourist destination than Mount Wilson, the railway carrying 3.1 million passengers before it closed in 1937.

Lowe built a hotel and the area's first observatory halfway up the line in 1894. Although the hotel burned down in 1900, the sixteen-inch telescope stayed in use for thirty-four years; more importantly, it established the precedent for thinking about Mount Wilson as an astronomy site. E. F. Spence, another former mayor of Los Angeles, had promised the University of Southern California fifty thousand dollars toward the construction of what would be the world's largest telescope, one with a forty-inch lens. USC sought the advice of the Harvard College Observatory in the matter of locating such an instrument atop Mount Wilson. Sending out an optical team, Harvard tested the site in January 1889 and, by spring of that year, had installed a thirteen-inch refractor there. At the same time, a group of Pasadena businessmen started work on a toll road up the mountain.

Harvard abandoned the site after only eighteen months because of the severe winter weather and isolation; the worsening economy of the region led to sale of the glass for the lens to astronomer George Hale, who represented the Yerkes Observatory in Wisconsin. Hale was interested in observing the sun and had invented the spectroheliograph, a device that could take a picture of the sun in any wavelength. Soon, however, Hale was bumping up against the observational limits of existing instruments, and he needed larger apertures to gather enough light to analyze the spectra of much more distant stars.

The earlier telescopes had all been refractors, in essence giant versions of the telescopes we use as kids. Refractor telescopes have at the front a large lens that focuses light down a tube to a smaller lens, the eyepiece, at the rear. The limitation of refractors is that a lens wider than forty inches in diameter becomes too heavy to support itself unless it is so thick that it begins to lose its ability to efficiently transmit light. That's not so much of a problem when you're making observations of bright objects relatively close, such as the sun or planets, but it severely cramps your style when you are attempting to observe objects outside the solar system. The larger instrument would have to be a reflecting one, which uses mirrors as its primary elements to focus the light into an eyepiece. Sir Isaac Newton invented the reflecting telescope in 1668, and he also first suggested putting telescopes on mountain peaks.

Basically, Hale was inventing the field of astrophysics, whereby the direct observations of astronomy are combined with the theoretical projections of physics to tackle such issues as the composition of stars and the physical structure of the universe. Like other branches of physics dealing with fundamental issues, the discipline demands ever more powerful tools. Eventually, astrophysics and its instruments would grow large enough to study the origins of the universe, an endeavor in which Mount Wilson would play a critical role. In the meantime, however, Hale decided to visit Mount Wilson for himself, a prime clear-air mountaintop property close to a major city.

Hale made his first trip up Mount Wilson in June 1903 with the director of the Lick Observatory, which had been built earlier on a mountaintop near San Jose, almost three hundred miles to the north. The first major mountaintop observatory in the country and the first permanently occupied mountain observatory anywhere, Lick was a model to at least consider for a new facility. Starting out from Pasadena, where the skies were covered in the low clouds typical of the seasonal "June gloom" marine layer creeping in from the coast, the two men were pessimistic about their chances of being able to test the site. But, as is also usual for those conditions, the party climbed up out of the inversion and into sunshine. A nine-inch telescope was set up on the summit, and Hale made his first solar observations from the mountain. A year later, he signed a ninety-nine-year lease with the Mount Wilson Toll Road Company, and six years later, a sixty-inch reflector was installed. In 1917, the hundred-inch Hooker reflector was added, setting the stage for the arrival of an ambitious young astronomer named Edwin Hubble at the controls of the world's largest eye into the universe.

The first of the two large telescopes installed by Hale was a remarkably successful instrument that continues to work to this day. Partly its success stems from the quality of its optics and its sturdiness of construction—an old saying among astronomers is that a telescope is something the size and weight of a bridge built to the specifications of a Swiss watch. But its dependability is also due to the unique and ongoing atmospheric conditions at Mount Wilson. The skies are clear around three hundred days a year; this was the first solar observatory, oddly enough, to be built in a sunny climate. Second, although the metropolitan area was quickly filling in below the San Gabriels even during the 1920s, the range sits next to the stabilizing influence of the ocean waters, which moderate temperature swings and diurnal atmospheric disturbances, helping further preserve those thermal inversions that trap the marine layer like a lid over the lights. It was the superior light-gathering power of the larger instrument in combination with the clear and steady air that let Hubble recognize that he was seeing beyond our own galaxy.

The blank for the hundred-inch mirror, like that of the earlier sixty-inch, had been cast in the Saint-Gobain glassworks factory outside Paris. Saint-Gobain was responsible for making most of the world's wine bottles, the only facility in the world capable of shaping into a disk a blob of molten glass that weighed more than nine thousand pounds. The blank arrived in Pasadena in December 1908, and after years of patient shaping and polishing, and then a coating with silver, the reflector was delivered to Mount Wilson in July 1917. It received its first light on the evening of November 1 of that year. The eighteen-inch-thick mirror, which is now recoated annually with aluminum, a material that does not tarnish as readily as silver, remains the largest solid plate-glass mirror in the world. (The instrument to displace the Hooker as the world's largest telescope, the two-hundred-inch reflector atop Mount Palomar, which opened in 1947, was made possible only by honeycombing its 14.5-ton Pyrex mirror.)

Hubble had studied astronomy at the University of Chicago and worked at Yerkes, but despite being inspired by Hale, Hubble turned his energies first to studying law, then to attempting to participate in World War I. Fortunately for us, he was too late. When the six-foot-two, pipe-smoking thirty-year-old astronomer showed up at Mount Wilson in late 1919, having recently mustered out of the army, he was still wearing his major's uniform and a belted trench coat. He quickly resumed his role as a scientist, however, and by Christmas Eve was seated at the controls. Interested in studying the structure of nebulae, or clouds of gas inside the Milky Way, Hubble set to photographing them with long exposures. Because most nebulae are so distant and faint, their internal features are not discernible through direct observation, but only through the accumulation of photons on a photosensitive plate over a period of minutes or hours.

On October 5, 1923, Hubble took a forty-five-minute-long exposure of what was then called the Andromeda Nebula. The scientist saw stars that appeared to wax and wane from plate to plate. By carefully examining those stars in which the relative brightness oscillated at precise intervals, Hubble could measure their distance. What he saw on this particular exposure was proof that the nebula was not a cloud inside our galaxy, but instead a separate aggregation of stars, the Andromeda Galaxy, and that the universe was a much bigger place than had been previously thought. Hubble published his results in 1924, then followed them up in 1927 with observations that showed the universe was expanding in all directions, thus laying the groundwork for all current theories about the Big Bang.

If you walk on the one-lane private road that goes west from the Hooker and down toward "the Monastery," the forty-room dormitory used by astronomers, you'll find a small bronze plaque next to a stubby concrete pillar. Although the view is now screened by small oak trees and brush, this spot is where, at the same time that Hubble was photographing nebulae, the Nobel Prize–winning physicist Albert Michelson was remeasuring the speed of light. Michelson had been experimenting with light since the previous century and had always hoped to be able to calculate its speed. In the 1880s, he had conducted a famous series of experiments that enabled Albert Einstein two decades later to formulate the theory of relativity. Now, in 1924, Michelson was atop Mount Wilson to measure as precisely as possible the speed of light as it bounced from the summit to that of Mount San Antonio. The U.S. Coast and Geodetic Survey first measured off the 22-mile distance to within 2.5 centimeters of error, at the time the most accurate survey ever made on the planet's surface. Michelson then spent more than two years reflecting light back and forth between the two peaks. When he was done in 1926, he had pinned down the speed of light to within plus or minus 6 kilometers per second to roughly its currently accepted value of 299,792 kilometers per second, or 186,282 miles per second.

Hubble, along with his colleagues and the telescopes on Mount Wilson, made two great discoveries that changed our entire conception of space, which Einstein acknowledged when he visited him in Pasadena during 1931. By proving that we were living in a solar system in a far-flung arm of the Milky Way, just one galaxy among billions of such islands in the universe—and that the universe was expanding uniformly in all directions—Hubble ushered in a profound shift in human relationships with nature, again moving us further from a homocentric view of the universe.

Michelson and Hubble were also vastly expanding our

understanding of time and how deep it extends into the past.
When you look at an image of the sun from the 150-foot-tall
solar tower on Mount Wilson, you're looking at light that has
traveled 92,960,000 miles in eight minutes; in other words, you're
seeing something that happened eight minutes ago. When you
see Proxima Centauri, the nearest star, you are looking 4.2 years
back in time (because the star is 4.2 light-years, or about 24.8
trillion miles, away in space). Hubble, when capturing images
from Andromeda, was crossing 2 million years back in time.
And now, when we look close to what we think is the edge of
the universe, we're gazing back to within 500,000 years of the
Big Bang, that progenitive expansion 13.7 billion years ago.

Michelson's measurements were dealing with time on a small
scale, the light bouncing back and forth between the two mountain peaks being, from a human perspective, an almost instanta-
neous event. But for the truly enormous distances that Hubble
was dealing with, the time it takes light to travel from star to
star was the only feasible way of compressing the numbers into
comprehensibility. In addition, Einstein had demonstrated how
light shifts toward the red end of the visible spectrum when
its source is receding from us. Hubble, using Einstein's and
Michelson's work, was able to see how large the universe really
was, which meant how old as well.

As I noted previously, we perceive time as having duration
and sequence. Duration measured over more than a few generations ceases to have much personal meaning for us, and we
can more readily understand the deep past through the use of
sequences. We may not be able to remember much, if anything,
about our great-great-grandparents, but we can visualize a family genealogy, its layers growing wider and wider as we go back

in time. We might not remember the names of the geological ages that preceded our own, but we can hold a core of sandstone drilled from the L.A. Basin, we can read the lines in it as seashores from 20 million years ago, and we can see how this fits into a geological sequence that leads not only up to the present, but also back to the formation of the earth 4.6 billion years ago.

We use another technique of compression when the numbers involved in measuring space get too large; we translate them into light speed and time, the only way we have of coping with the size of where we live.

The Mount Wilson Observatory has several challenges today in keeping up its status as a world-class astrophysics center, even though it has added newer instruments over the years. Light pollution from the L.A. Basin, for instance, reduces the amount of darkness to that of a night of a full moon, which is less than ideal for viewing, even though Mount Wilson still has some of the thermally steadiest air in North America. And bigger telescopes have been built, starting with the 200-inch reflector at Palomar Observatory ninety miles to the south, and more recently with the twin 394-inch Keck telescopes atop the dormant 13,800-foot Mauna Kea volcano on the island of Hawaii. The Keck instruments, one built in 1992 and the other in 1996, use adaptive optics—powerful lasers that shine up into the atmosphere to help show how light is being bounced around in the atmosphere, with computers then fine-tuning supplementary mirrors up to one hundred times a second. Adaptive optics makes these earthbound telescopes so sensitive that they can be used to conduct geological mapping of asteroids. Soon the

Keck telescopes will be linked through interferometry, which will give the astronomers the resolving power equivalent to a telescope with a 3,350-inch primary mirror.

Interferometry is currently the most sophisticated use of telescopes we have invented, a subject in which Lu Rarogie-wicz once gave me a crash course while standing next to the University of Georgia's Center for High Angular Resolution Astronomy (CHARA) building. The football-field-size building houses CHARA, a project that brings together the light from various combinations of six 40-inch telescopes set out in a Y pattern on the mountaintop, and as far away from each other as nearly eight hundred feet. Rarogiewicz, a pixielike gentleman with shoulder-length white hair, now serves as postmaster for Mount Wilson. He once ran one of the smaller interferometers there during the 1980s, when he held the world's record for resolving the diameters of stellar objects six years in a row.

In 1892, Michelson invented an interferometer that measured objects down to one second of arc—an instrument he used at the Lick Observatory to determine the size of the moons of Jupiter. His twenty-foot model installed atop the Hooker in 1920 consisted of a long metal track holding two mirrors that reflected light to a common point, where alignment and observation of the interference pattern of the light waves enabled him to measure the first stellar diameters outside our solar system. He determined the size of what appear to us from the ground to be the seven largest stars before he reached the limits of his tool. Michelson built a fifty-foot interferometer, but couldn't obtain the mechanical rigidity required to observe the "fringes" produced by the meeting of the beams that were only 0.00001 inch (one-hundred-thousandth of an inch) wide, and it wasn't

until 1978 that a graduate student built the next optical interferometer on the mountain.

The second modern interferometer on Mount Wilson was
built by Mike Shao in 1985. It could move its mirrors up to 103
feet apart and was so sensitive that it could measure down to
one-thousandth of an arc, a sensitivity that had applications to
terrestrial geology as well as stellar physics. Used to determine
how fast the San Gabriels were moving in relation to earthquake
faults, the instrument, Rarogiewicz noted with glee, "could
measure the mountaintop moving as little as fifty-thousandths
of an inch—we could see Mount Wilson move when a vehicle
braked on it!"

CHARA would soon begin using its six linked instruments
to obtain one hundred times the resolution of the Hubble Space
Telescope, which was currently providing our sharpest images
of deep space. The combined instruments would be able to
resolve features as small as a nickel from ten thousand miles
away—or a rock one foot across on the surface of the moon.
Light beams from the telescopes are bounced in a near vacuum
through long, white plastic pipes into the CHARA building,
a double-shelled structure. The outer wall provides insulation
from temperature changes, the inner one a "clean" environment
where the beams are aligned and observed.

The human eye needs between five and fifteen photons to
experience light. Because a pigment in the eye—rhodopsin, the
chemical that enables us to see at low light levels—is constantly
breaking down and emitting a photon when each of its molecules comes apart, the brain is programmed to ignore light
until it accumulates several photons at once. Still, five photons
is an exquisite sensitivity, in theory enough to see a single candle

flame burning twenty miles away under perfect conditions. Yet the CHARA interferometers, by collating light from what is a virtual mirror a fifth of a mile across, can resolve objects three hundred thousand times fainter than what the eye can see.

That's not to mention, of course, the computer linking of ten radio telescopes across North America that will soon act as if it were a single telescope five thousand miles across. What instruments of such resolving power give us is the ability not just to see other stars as a point of light, but to construct pictures of them as disks with visible features—and to observe how the black holes in the centers of other galaxies direct the flow of interstellar gases. The interferometers let us image structure, in other words, measure change over time.

The telescope was invented around 1609; the refracting telescope that Galileo used to look at the moon had a lens five centimeters (a hair under two inches) in diameter; the linked radio telescopes have a virtual aperture of eight thousand kilometers. That's an increase in size of 160 million times in less than four hundred years.

As large an accomplishment as that is, it pales next to the increase across the wavelengths that we can now observe. We can now detect the entire electromagnetic spectrum, from the shortest—gamma rays and X-rays—through the infrared, to microwave background radiation left over from the Big Bang, and all the way up to the longest radio waves, which propagate at six miles from crest to crest. The *Encyclopedia Britannica* puts the size of this spectrum as follows. If the slice of electromagnetism visible to our eyes, which is in the middle of the spectrum, were as thick as a single page in the encyclopedia, the width of the entire spectrum would stretch from Earth to the sun—in both directions. That's an increase of a million

billion times in each direction, a number we can understand
even dimly only by creating such similes.

Despite our expanded ability to measure the wide electromagnetic spectrum well enough to collect signals from near the
edge of our particular known universe and hence observe very
nearly its beginning, the populace of L.A. is more isolated than
ever from direct knowledge of its place in time and space. During the 1992 riots, when large portions of the city were blacked
out, people reportedly called up police stations in a panic to
ask what was wrong with the sky. It wasn't the smoke and fire
they were so worked up about—it was the Milky Way. They'd
never seen it before.

Two icons of astronomy and the larger universe are visible
from throughout much of Los Angeles: the white domes atop
Mount Wilson and the more retro verdigris ones in Griffith
Park. The white ones are dwarfed by the telecommunication
towers, and the Griffith Park domes are more likely to remind
residents of the movies than of astronomy, as the observatory/
planetarium has been a favorite location ever since James Dean
was filmed there in the classic 1955 film *Rebel Without a Cause*.
Ironically, that film's major scene set in the planetarium is a
lecture about the history of space and time.

Of course, being human, we don't just look at the increased
spectrum, but also use more and more of it, taking for granted
that bandwidth is just another territory of nature available for
colonization, the amassing of capital, and recreation. We sub-
divide bandwidth by assigning frequencies all along the spectrum as if it were land, then auction it off to the highest bidder
and tax the profits from its use. Telescopes are merely passive
receivers of the electromagnetic spectrum, just as the Hollywood

sign is only a passive transmitter of information. But we now swim in great pools and streams of electromagnetism that we actively generate for everything from transmitting pop music to cooking food in the kitchen.

If you look at a spreadsheet of the spectrum from just 30 to 6,400 megahertz (30 MHz to 64 GHz), the part of the spectrum where radio does its business, you can see how densely we crowd parts of it. The signal you get on your beeper is broadcast at the low end, 35–36 MHz. At the high end, you're into military and weather radar and airplane navigation frequencies. In between is a bewildering array of activity. The bandwidth of 50–54 MHz is where my father hung out as an amateur radio operator. And 54–72 MHz is set aside for television channels 2 through 4; just above that are the frequencies commonly used by radio astronomers. FM radio stations broadcast at 88–108 MHz, where the wavelengths are typically only ten feet long and antennae must be adjusted carefully to transmit and receive signals. (AM stations broadcast way down around 535–1,605 kilohertz, where wavelengths are measured in hundreds of yards and a coat hanger will work as an antenna.)

Things get most crowded from 1,755 MHz, which carries everything from remote-controlled military weapons to satellite telemetry, through the Space Band used by the National Aeronautics and Space Administration (NASA), and the microwave frequencies (2,400–2,690 MHz). The microwave bandwidths are used by cordless phones, cordless speakers, wireless cable TV, and, yes, your microwave oven. (Stick your head into an FM radio station transmitting facility up on Mount Wilson, and your brain will literally start to warm up ever so slightly.) There is not, in fact, any more room for broadcasting in the microwave section of the spectrum, just as there's no more land on Mount Wilson to expand the boundaries of the radio frequency forest, or RF jungle, as it's sometimes called, and the property values of the real and virtual estates are rising fast.

As I walked back down the narrow roads from the telescopes to the telecommunication towers on the peak, the contrast between the two kinds of structures was arresting. The telescopes are devoted to collecting light from millions and billions of years ago, measuring space in such magnitudes that only the speed of light can convey the distances. They are thus engaged in collecting time photon by photon and analyzing it as a fundamental feature of the universal continuum. The towers, on the other hand, are about the diminution of time. Using increasingly shorter wavelengths to broadcast information around the basin, the antennae are devoted to instantaneity, to everyone's experiencing the world in "real time," what is advertised by phone and personal communications companies as the here and now with no delay.

Perhaps the most starkly visible urban telecommunication tower in America is the one atop Sutro Hill in San Francisco. Built in 1973 and measuring in at 970 feet, it dominates the horizon line of the western Bay Area. Constructed, as usual, to overcome the obstacle that terrain presents to profit, in this case the hills of the San Francisco Peninsula to the television stations of the city, the tower stands behind one of America's most romantic skylines like a gawky transformer robot in a science fiction cartoon. Even at its monstrous height, however, it is nowhere near the height of the 1,500-foot tower in Cedar Hill, Texas. The Texas structure collapsed in October 1996 while it was being repaired during a windstorm. Serving television

stations in the Dallas–Fort Worth area, it was the tallest structure west of the Mississippi River, 50 feet taller than the Sears
Tower in Chicago.

Mount Wilson, however, is a world-renowned supersite
among antennae farms. Its RF jungle hosts hundreds of antennae mounted on dozens of towers, many of which are as much
as 400 feet tall. Television shows, like the ones taped behind Park
La Brea at the CBS Studio City, are beamed up to the mountain
via microwave for rebroadcast over the region. The signals are
received by large dishes on the buildings, channeled into the
transmitting facilities, where the signals are then boosted up
in power and sent by cable up the towers, from where they're
beamed out to your family TV set. The first live television
newscast was broadcast from Mount Wilson by KTLA in the
year of my birth, 1949, far before most of the country had access
to television of any kind. And in 1952, the station arranged for
TV signals to be hopscotched on mountain peaks clear from the
Nevada Test Site to provide Los Angelenos with a live broadcast of an atomic bomb test, not only a technical feat of some
magnitude, but also a shockwave in the national psyche.

Seven television stations and twelve FM radio stations were
among the customers renting space on the mountain when I
was visiting, their antennae sitting 6,000 feet above sea level,
about 5,500 feet over most of Los Angeles. The antennae stand
an average of 3,000 feet above the steep ridges and other peaks
of the surrounding terrain and can broadcast over five thousand
square miles. Line-of-sight signals broadcast from here reach
as far as ninety-six miles to the south before they fall off the
curvature of the earth out over the Pacific Ocean.

You can drive along the bases of the antennae, but not

approach too closely, because many of the structures are fenced off. One of the reasons for the barrier is that the towers do emit significant amounts of radio frequency radiation (RFR), enough that prolonged exposure directly in the path of the broadcast can cook your eyeballs and reproductive organs. If you're a worker repairing gear on a tower and ignoring the work safety regulations, you'd probably have to push yourself to accumulate enough exposure to hurt something, but liability laws being what they are, no chances are taken to allow the public a bath in the beams.

According to the Federal Communications Commission (FCC), more than fourteen thousand radio and television stations were on the air in the United States in 1999, and all of them required antennae to broadcast. Most of the VHF and UHF channels in the Los Angeles Basin have transmitters on Mount Wilson, but the granddaddy of them all is the CBS tower. Don Lee, the man for whom the peak by Griffith Park is named, first brought a tower to the site in 1950 to broadcast Channel 2. After a dispute with the FCC, a 400-foot tower was eventually erected. A major problem, however, was that much of the San Gabriel and San Bernardino valleys, being hidden behind various ridges, wasn't able to receive the signal. A series of photographs comparing the lines of sight from 400 and 900 feet above the ridge was made, demonstrating to the station's executives how they would gain hundreds of thousands of viewers by extending the height. While the other towers on the peak are regulated by the U.S. Forest Service and are restricted to a maximum height of 400 feet, in part to limit potential interference with the observatories, the CBS facility is located on its own land and is far enough to the northwest that it was allowed

to top out at 975 feet. More than 10 million people in the basin
now get its signal, 7 million of them simply by pointing rabbit
ears at Mount Wilson.

The tower is a pivot-pin type, its steel foot resting in a cup
that allows the structure to twist and sway with the wind—
enough to maintain structural integrity but not disrupt the signal. While standing next to the open cup and trying to ignore
the fact that 1.5 million pounds of thrust was being directed
downward by the tower to within a few feet of my kneecaps, I
noticed that every structure nearby was covered with industrial-
gauge steel-grate awnings. During the winter, chunks of ice the
size of Volkswagens fall off the tower and onto the grills, which
slice and dice the chunks into ice cubes before the debris hits
anything valuable—like the cables carrying the signals from the
transmitter to the tower, not to mention the engineers.

Apart from a construction crew working on a new tower
and transmitting building, Mount Wilson on a weekday was
a quiet spot. Occasionally, a busload of schoolchildren might
be delivered to the observatories for a tour, but the telecommunications areas were relatively deserted. And getting more
so all the time. Substantial crews used to be stationed up there
on rotating shifts twenty-four hours a day, but now everything
is monitored increasingly by long distance. An engineer sitting
down in Los Angeles monitors everything on a computer, using
a touch-tone phone to change power levels or other necessary
variables up at the transmitter. Soon it will be possible to issue
just voice commands, and the skeleton crews left up here may
have to make only sporadic visits. Unlike the astronomers who
sleep at the Monastery, which is divided into daytime and night-
time sleeping accommodations, the telecommunications engineers can go home.

Personally, I find the antennae on Mount Wilson romantic, no doubt in part because my father was an avid shortwave radio operator and his small laboratory, where he did research on radar under contract for the U.S. Navy, had a radio mast of its own. Sitting on a tall stool in the lab at night with him, I watched the green faces of oscilloscopes glow with their elaborate and hypnotic exhibitions of waveforms going in and out of phase. As he talked to other radio operators around the world, I felt as if I were living a science fiction story. The mixture of astronomy and telecommunications on Mount Wilson remains a potent one for me, and I was definitely melancholy when driving back down the mountain.

There are, to be sure, plenty of antennae to see in L.A., but they lack the majesty of the big towers broadcasting radio and television signals. The L.A. antennae are the rapidly proliferating monopoles of the cellular communications industry, which hosts a series of short rods standing vertically in a circle around their tops. Cellular communications broadcast at relatively low energy levels out to a small radius, sometimes just a few city blocks, and thus require many more antennae. One of the joys of living in L.A. was always to keep an eye out for cell-phone conversations in improbable places, so common a phenomenon now that it's no longer even a pop culture cliché. Equally ordinary now are pairs of people walking down the street talking on cell phones instead of to each other. And every one of those phones is being served by an antenna within a few blocks.

By the end of 2000, cell towers were going up in L.A. at the rate of three per week, and well over a thousand towers were already within city limits. Across America, the FCC tallied more than 73,000 cell-phone towers taller than two hundred feet (and more than a hundred 100-cell sites with shorter antennae mounted on rooftops and poles). As long as the telecommunications industry was limited to radio and television broadcasting, which usually meant antennae located with sightlines to the home receiving units, hence up on ridges and in open fields away from homes, people put up with the new Erector set constructions, which often imitated the oil derricks in appearance. But with the advent of wireless personal communications that required thickets of stubby antennae towers within neighborhoods, public opposition grew. Now it was the view out the bedroom window that was threatened.

And this was related to why the oil derricks were disguised around town; as the residential areas of the city expanded, the derricks were considered gauche reminders of industry, an ungainly tribe of machines plunked down in paradise. The communication towers on the ridgelines, by contrast, were a manifestation of the power that broadcast media, the unique product of Hollywood, was exercising over the world. They signaled modernity, a new kind of industry in which the town was, for the most part, a proud and willing collaborator. The cell towers are nothing so heroic, however, more an appliance than a romantic allusion.

The solutions began to get ingenious. Cell towers were being hidden in bell towers and church steeples, and camouflaged to look like pine trees everywhere from Memphis to Los Angeles. And in Arizona, suspiciously symmetrical, thirty-five-foot-tall saguaro cacti appeared overnight. Apart from the controversies over the adverse health effects that may or may not result someday from the thousandfold increase in a year of microwave radiation in cities such as Los Angeles, the antennae make visible a massive disruption of how we experience time. The duration of events is shortened and segmented by constant and unexpected phone calls, and the sequencing of events likewise altered.

This is, of course, perfect for a place like Los Angeles, where life seems more often than in other cities to be construed by citizens in short, episodic sequences interrupted by even shorter and denser serial, but nonsequential, episodes. Which is to say, when driving down Wilshire Boulevard and talking on a cell phone doing a deal, you may find that the segmentation of your life resembles more than not a television show with commercials. This is a phenomenon not limited anymore to the Southern California megalopolis, as any traveler can tell you. Where and when goes L.A., so goes the rest of the world, the city's ideas and lifestyles spread planetwide through broadcast media and movies. The electromagnetic feeding frenzy born with television in Los Angeles has been carried to even more extreme in countries such as Japan and Finland, where the use of cell phones was adopted even earlier and more pervasively.

The weekend after visiting Mount Wilson, I was feeling nostalgic for a classic tower, so I returned to Mount Lee. The peak is home to both a telecommunications facility and the Hollywood sign, the latter being a world-renowned tourist attraction, although I never saw tourists any closer than several miles away, their telephoto zoom lenses in action. Getting near the sign requires a bit of a hike, and when standing above it on Mount Lee Drive (an access road that only official vehicles are allowed to drive up), you're warned by a sign that this is a Mountain Fire District and that no hiking down to the sign is permitted. Like the telecommunication tower, the sign is fenced off.

It was one of those days when the marine layer had cleared,

but the basin was still full of haze and smog. I couldn't see past
the houses at the bottom of the park, though I could hear the
traffic on the freeways like a distant waterfall that rose and fell
in volume as I rounded each bend in the ridge. Once, I heard a
train, which must have been miles away down below, its horn
as clear as if it were right in front of me, the sound perhaps
bouncing off a thermal cap above the city.

The telecommunications tower atop Mount Lee, which is
painted in the alternating bands of red and white required by
the Federal Aviation Authority, is just as impressive as the CBS
tower atop Mount Wilson. Even though the Mount Lee structure is little more than three hundred feet tall, it's the only
tower on the peak and has a commanding presence. Originally
erected in 1939, it was the first television transmission tower
in L.A., necessitated by the fact that Los Angeles is the only
major metropolitan area in the world bisected by a mountain
range. The Hollywood Hills and Santa Monicas divide the Los
Angeles Basin from the San Fernando Valley, and the easiest
way to get signals from one place to the other is with an array
of antennae on the most convenient high spot in between.
Designed as one of the derrick-style towers that cropped up
all over town in the 1920s, when there was still an oil boom, the
original was replaced with the current structure in 1996, which
copied the old design, more because it had proven stable in the
hundred-mile-an-hour Santa Anas than out of any historical
or metaphorical propriety.

The structure is securely fenced and monitored by surveil-
lance cameras, but I was able to count at least ninety-six antennae of various kinds mounted on it, although I couldn't see
all of them at any one time. A sign posted on the electric gate
notes, "Beyond this point: Radio frequency fields at this site

exceed the FCC rules for human exposure," and that trespass "could result in serious injury." In a separate exclosure, nine video cameras mounted on poles are pointed at the city, remote units used by various television stations for background feeds during weather reports.

Walking back down, I contemplated how static was the 50-foot-high and 450-foot-long "signal" of the Hollywood sign, versus the very active signals coming from the antennae on the tower, a structure that in most photographs is carefully cropped out of the frame. The sign was originally erected in 1923 as an advertisement, reading "Hollywoodland." The last four letters were removed by the Hollywood Chamber of Commerce in 1945. Everything possible since then has been done to preserve the sign, including an upgrade in its construction from wood to corrugated metal. The chamber is not shy about prosecuting people who attempt unauthorized physical alteration of its image.

The sign has graduated from the status of those white initials you see painted by high school students on hillsides above towns in the West, half geographical locators and half symbols of local civic pride, to occupying a place of privilege among international icons such as the Eiffel Tower and the Empire State Building. As a logotype and architectonic totem, the sign is, of course, more appropriate for Los Angeles than an actual building, because the town is built on facade as much as foundation. Where other cities have adopted actual buildings as their symbols, Los Angeles quite properly embraced an advertisement. In turn, the sign represents a conflation of the city, the place, with its products, which are beamed around the globe. Of course the sign should reside next to a telecommunication tower, which itself symbolizes the broadcasting of images and commerce, a significance apparently lost on the postcard companies.

I looked across to Mount Wilson, the antennae atop which were clearly visible above the layer of brown haze filling the San Fernando Valley. Below me on the north of Mount Lee was one of the Forest Lawn Memorial Parks and possibly an old landfill, a large, scruffy acreage curiously undeveloped and adjacent to both the cemetery and the park. I thought about how we bring petroleum up out of the ground and how we transmit waves through the air—and I wondered about what we put back in the ground. I decided it was time to come down from the hills and visit my great-grandmother, who passed away in the early 1950s. Surely she would have something to tell me about the nature of time in Los Angeles.

LANDFILLING

After my sojourn up Mount Lee, I rummaged around in the family strongbox for the cemetery papers. Inside an envelope with a Forest Lawn Memorial Parks return address was a receipt made out to William Henry Lyman, my great-grandfather, who in 1927 paid what was then the enormous sum of $4,500 for a private crypt. Also enclosed was a "Deed and Certificate of Perpetual Care" from nine years later, papers that had been prepared for my great-grandmother, his wife and the grand dame of my childhood. She had been forced to buy a larger crypt and authorize the shuffling about of bodies to accommodate the body of her son—who had died unexpectedly while on a cruise in the South China Sea—next to the remains of her now-deceased husband.

Forest Lawn Cemetery started out in 1906 as a modest fifty-five-acre plot of chaparral and eucalyptus trees at the corner of San Fernando Road and Glendale Avenue, a major crossroads in a town that, the same year, would incorporate as the city of Glendale. A scraggly operation, the cemetery was nonetheless ideally situated less than ten miles from downtown and near where Henry Huntington would run a railway line for commuters. In the 1920s, as the L.A. Basin was undergoing its oil boom, Glendale claimed the title of being the fastest-growing city in America, gaining as many as ten thousand residents in one year alone. Today, it's the third-largest city in the county (after Los Angeles itself and Long Beach).

Hubert Eaton, an emigrant from Missouri who had lost his shirt investing in a Nevada silver mine, took up the position of cemetery sales manager at Forest Lawn in 1912 to repay his backers. He may have been a lousy miner, but he was a brilliant salesman of graveyard plots. Having seen in Missouri how cemetery property could be sold "before need," he was the first person to apply the concept west of the Mississippi. Within three years, he was moving so much acreage that he bought into the company, and within five, he was made general manager, which meant he was now in charge of how the place actually looked—and Eaton had some specific ideas.

Cemeteries in America weren't divorced from churchyards until the overcrowding among their dead within city limits became so severe that decomposing bodies created odoriferous miasmas that seeped through the city streets. The gas was thought to bear disease, but unlike methane or hydrogen sulfide, which could have posed genuine health threats, the stench of the corpses mostly just infected civic populations with a mass gag reflex. Consequently, a rural-cemetery movement started up in the early nineteenth century. Featuring discreet glades screened by rows of trees, a design modeled after picturesque English landscape designs, the properties were crossed by winding roads and, by the mid-1800s, began to feature historical monuments. Some of the cemeteries would annually attract up to one hundred thousand visitors, who came not so much to pay their respects to the dead as to experience a bit of nature that had been artfully cultivated around history.

Cemetery comes from the Greek word for "sleeping chamber," and the classical *campo santo* found in Italy was a graveyard built on top of earth brought back during the Crusades from the Holy Land. In America, once separated from the churches, cemeteries were our first theme parks. Today, there are as many as one hundred thousand European-style cemeteries in America, and Forest Lawn is accorded status as one of the most influential in the development of the industry, not least because of the change signified by the revision of its name from a cemetery to a "memorial park." Young Eaton envisioned a literalization of the Glendale facility's name: a hillside park of rolling lawns with discrete sightlines and uplifting vistas framed by tall evergreens that would signify everlasting life. The only problem was the tombstones, which he considered a gloomy distraction from his plans for an inspirational setting. Perhaps the entrepreneur also had in mind an eminently practical reason, an economy afforded by the gasoline-powered, mechanical mowing of grass. He was told he wouldn't be able to get rid of the native Southern California weeds and maintain a green lawn, much less a forest of pine trees. But with the help of intensive hand labor and somewhat primitive tractors, he conquered the local devil grass, established a tree farm, and, to irrigate the grounds, availed himself of the spigot William Mulholland had opened up for the development of the San Fernando Valley. That was the easy part.

The hard part was getting rid of headstones and substituting bronze plaques set flush with the ground, as it involved overcoming the resistance of two powerful groups of people: the customers, who couldn't imagine eternal rest without a granite marker memorializing their location, and the monument-manufacturing industry, which considered the proposal unfair restraint of trade and sued in court to prevent the sacrilege. Eaton won, but only by instituting a 10 percent discount for customers who would give up their monument privileges. The bottom line won out over what was, after all, only a theoretical immortality.

Eaton's ambitions for Forest Lawn were just beginning,

however. As soon as World War I was over, he boarded a ship and scoured Europe for examples of classical sculpture and antiquities that would make manifest what he called the "memorial impulse," the inclination of people to forestall oblivion by erecting artistic structures to preserve their legacy. Think of the Pyramids and the Taj Mahal.

In 1915, he bought the first sculpture for the property, a sentimental bronze of a naked baby girl holding two ducklings. Eaton regarded his memorial park as a place to celebrate life as well as death, the beginnings as well as the endings. From this distance in time, it's hard to assess what part his own emotions played in this decision. In any case, the rebalancing of his clients' collective mood away from grief and toward celebration was good enough for business that he could afford to build the largest collections of marble statuary and stained-glass windows in America. More than nine hundred statues are scattered throughout the five cemeteries that now make up the Forest Lawn regional chain of memorial parks, in addition to two hundred bronzes and five hundred stained-glass windows. Many of the marbles are copies of notable European works by artists such as Raphael and Michelangelo. In fact, literature published by the company boasts that some of its replicas are carved out of white Carrara marble from the same quarries used by Michelangelo and that nowhere else in the world is it possible to view as many copies of his great works in one place.

Then there was the question of buildings. Like the art, the architecture would be inspired by important buildings throughout Europe. Eaton started in 1917 with a modest structure modeled closely after the English church where the poet Thomas Gray wrote "Elegy Written in a Country Churchyard." In a fit of inspired romanticism, the businessman added an indoor garden and singing canaries. The themed building was so popular with couples that they soon began requesting to be married there, a practice Forest Lawn initiated in 1923, creating yet another revenue stream. Baptisms were added soon thereafter. Over the next seventy years, more than sixty thousand people were married in the eight churches on Forest Lawn properties.

By the late 1920s, Forest Lawn had one million dollars in sales annually, had hosted more than twenty-eight thousand interments, and was employing a staff of four hundred to handle the remains of 3,600 people each year—and conducting nine hundred weddings. It was becoming apparent to Eaton that Forest Lawn could profitably open a mortuary, thus creating a complete life-to-death service center. The problem was that cemeteries and mortuaries were considered two kinds of enterprises, thus allowing the death industry to squeeze grieving relatives twice, once for the transportation and preparation of the body and casket, then again for burial. Kickbacks between mortuaries and the cemeteries they favored were common. Eaton, again applying his genius for increasing economy of operations, fought on several fronts during the early 1930s to bring this last service onto the premises. Battling the State Board of Funeral Directors and their national association, as well as the California State Assembly, the Glendale City Council, and the casket makers, who were under threat of boycott from mortuaries across the country, Eaton finally prevailed in the courts in December 1933.

While the Depression was ending, but California still booming, Eaton and his board of directors began looking for a second site. In 1944, they purchased the 400 acres of the historic El Rancho Providencia, which in 1914 had been bought by Jesse Lasky, Cecil B. DeMille's partner, and turned into the location for D. W. Griffith's *Birth of a Nation, All Quiet on the Western Front,* and numerous Westerns. Once more, Eaton would take an undeveloped and hilly property and turn it into a theme park, this one based on an American colonial motif. Various shrines and activities would celebrate George Washington and Abraham Lincoln, then later the Mexican heritage of the area. No doubt Eaton was pleased that his new memorial park was located next to the largest municipal park in the country, the 4,044-square-acre Griffith Park. This Forest Lawn property was one of the two lawns I'd seen from Mount Lee.

A dairy farm in Cypress, a community to the south and on the border of Los Angeles and Orange counties, was converted into a third Forest Lawn facility in 1958; the Covina Hills branch to the east opened in 1965. The Sunnyside Memorial Gardens in Long Beach, a cemetery done up in Spanish colonial, had been in existence since 1900 but was failing. Forest Lawn purchased it in 1978 and completely renovated the facility.

Of course, I hadn't known much of this when standing on Mount Lee. My experiences with Forest Lawn in the past had consisted of driving by the Covina Hills property when using the Interstate 10 freeway to get into L.A. from Claremont, where I was going to college in the late 1960s. I had always assumed that this cemetery was *the* Forest Lawn, having no idea there were more than one. The only other thing I knew was that I had some papers relating to Great-Grandmother and her crypt sitting in a safe box under my desk at home. When looking down at the carefully arranged green geometry near Griffith Park, which was in total contrast to the wild chaparral of public lands, I knew I was looking at another Forest Lawn, one I assumed was probably the original and the location of Elizabeth Lyman's remains.

With the documents from the safe box in hand, I drove to the back side of Griffith Park, parked inside the tall gates of the cemetery, and walked over to the information booth, handing the deed through its window. The gentleman who accepted my bona fides was middle-aged and was wearing a gray polyester suit and a less-than-expensive tie. He read the description of the burial's whereabouts twice, pursed his lips, shook his head. His accent was middle European.

"No," he said, "the Mausoleum-Columbarium is at the Forest Lawn in Glendale. It's only ten minutes. Here, I will get you a map." He traced a line on a preprinted map without lifting his pen off the paper once, his practiced gesture letting me know that I had made no more than a common mistake. I told him that I wanted to drive around here, in any case, and he pointed out to me areas of interest I should visit.

"Here is my card, please. Call me if I can be of assistance. I can help you with a property in Glendale, not just here." As I turned away, he added: "And prices go up 20 or 30 percent per year." It was the same pitch, I realized, used by a Forest Lawn representative in a letter to my great-grandfather written in 1927. "V. Jon Longo—Before Need Counselor" read the card I was now holding.

I drove into the park, my objective to reach its far southeastern corner, where it looked as if a hillside was under development. Perhaps it was part of the landfill, I thought, but driving along the uppermost drive until I reached a dirt cul-de-sac and passing small signs that warned "No Trespassing—Dangerous Conditions," I found patches of green lawn inset with bronze plaques alternating with bare, scraped earth. The hillside, which rose upward and disappeared over its crest toward the boundary of Griffith Park, looked as though it had been prepared for development, shaved of the chaparral and awaiting earthmovers.

The telecommunication tower on Mount Lee stood far above. Power lines marched down over the hill in front of me, crossed the cemetery, and continued on down to the Los Angeles River and Interstate 5. I thought I knew where I was, but if this was a landfill, then it was one soon to be used by Forest Lawn. I got back in the car to trace what I could of Griffith Park on this, its northern, side.

Outside the gates and back on Forest Lawn Drive, I turned right and proceeded down to Mount Sinai Memorial Park, the Jewish cemetery next door. I didn't stop at the gates this time, but cruised in and up through its terraces, the subdivisions of the dead. A wide, white casket sat on a small trailer by an open hole cut into the highest level, presumably awaiting a party of mourners. I was tooling around on a path right below where I'd been in Forest Lawn. Back down the hill, another right turn, and I was at Griffith Park Drive, which I followed until I reached a recycling center for green waste. Above and to my right loomed the steep escarpment of what was unmistakably the Toyon Landfill, a hillside set back with multiple earthen benches and bearing large drainage pipes from the top. This was the other lawn I'd spied from atop Mount Lee.

Landfills, like cemeteries, are usually placed on what are initially the outskirts of town, then get encircled by development as, simultaneously, they are filled up with refuse from the new suburbs. In the United States, each person generates about 4 pounds of solid waste per day—that's more than 209 million tons per year nationwide. Roughly a hundred landfills reach capacity and are closed each year. And as the housing units and apartment complexes and strip malls become denser around the dumps, the need for green space also rises dramatically. Around the Los Angeles Basin and San Fernando Valley, several former landfills are slowly being converted, as they degas and settle, into recreational facilities. Golf courses, bicycle trails, soccer fields, and baseball diamonds are the major uses to which they are put. Toyon is no exception.

Created in the 1950s, but inactive as a dump since 1988, the Toyon Landfill hosted a four-hundred-foot-high pile of trash when it was closed, then covered with a layer of dirt. The place is expected to settle for about thirty years, at a rate of up to four feet annually in places, as its contents decompose. And as the trash in the garbage graveyard rots underneath, it generates methane as surely as if there were plankton down there. The Toyon Power Station atop the landfill converts the gas into an equivalent of 115,000 barrels of oil a day. The Penrose Landfill, near Tujunga Avenue, using a similar network of pipes and manifolds built into the layers of garbage, generates enough power to light ten thousand homes. I wondered briefly why we didn't treat bodies the same way, but, of course, I also remembered the difficulty our culture has with cremations, much less with harvesting the decomposing remains of people as an energy resource.

Burning the dead is an old practice, in European heritage dating back at least to the ancient Greeks three thousand years ago, but it's a practice many Christians throughout the centuries have considered pagan, so it has never been as popular in the West as inhumation in the ground. The two principal historical reasons used by Europeans to override their prejudice were the overcrowding of urban cemeteries and the control of disease. During the spread of bubonic plague, bodies were often disposed of in mass cremations, such as those in Naples in 1656, when the corpses of sixty thousand victims of the disease were burned.

In America, the first documented cremation was in 1792, but it wasn't until 1873 that a modern, enclosed crematory was built. In 1900–1901, only 5,107 cremations were reported in America, but by the time Forest Lawn's Great Mausoleum was built in 1920, there were seventy-four crematories in the country and the rate of cremation had more than doubled. Almost a quarter of the facilities, which reduced a body to ashes in a little more than an hour's time, were located in California, the most of any state—and Forest Lawn's huge building was also serving as a *columbarium,* or vault with niches for urns holding the ashes of the deceased. In 1999, according to the Cremation Association of North America, nearly 600,000 cremations took place, or just over 25 percent of the total number of deceased persons for that year. California remained the number one state for cremations, with slightly more than 103,000.

The most compelling modern argument in favor of cremations is their economy in comparison with traditional burials. Some twenty-two thousand funeral homes operate in America, a $12-billion-a-year industry that transports, transforms, and encloses bodies for burial. Funeral homes pick up the deceased from homes and hospitals, embalm or incinerate the bodies, and package them in everything from simple metal boxes to caskets costing upward of $10,000. The average cost of this service is $5,000. Burial runs another $2,000. Cremations are simply cheaper, running as little as $400.

The problem with cremations is that the modern natural-gas-fired ovens burn from 1,400°F to 1,800°F for thirty to sixty minutes to reduce a body down to three to nine pounds of bone fragments. The process produces carcinogenic dioxins, hydrochloric and hydrosulfuric acids, and carbon dioxide, all of which is of great interest to the people at the Environmental

Protection Agency (EPA), who are attempting to set regulatory air pollution standards for the industry. The EPA already requires large landfills, such as Toyon, to prevent leakage of toxic gases and liquids during that thirty-year degassing period. Most likely, the regulation of toxins from the disposal of bodies is not far behind.

I wondered, looking up at the mastaba-like slopes of the Toyon Landfill, why we don't at least compost bodies here as they do in England, where they conduct green burials in recycled organic containers that decompose with the body and fertilize trees in what are zoned as nature preserves. Although most of the landfills around L.A. are eventually turned into recreational parks, long a secondary use of cemeteries, I continued to ponder why we didn't also capture the energy from the cremations and sell it back to the power grid, as is done with the garbage. With such thoughts in mind, I drove to Glendale, only five minutes away.

Forest Lawn at Glendale was an entirely different proposition from the Hollywood Hills facility. Where the buildings and grounds of the memorial park under Mount Lee were in the open and the layout of the interments easily discernible, the original Glendale property was heavily wooded, its arrangement more discrete. An outsized English Tudor mansion just inside reputedly the world's largest iron gates was obviously the mortuary, but few other features were visible. Again I stopped at the information booth. This time the polite and suited gentleman inside, speaking in the same accent as his Hollywood counterpart, was being harassed by a man of indeterminate age, social station, and sanity. Carrying a paper bag with a pair of women's white pumps peeking out, the visitor weaved gently from side to side, inquiring about both the cheapest and the most expensive plots available, and periodically interjecting a request for a bar. The Forest Lawn representative was unflaggingly polite, answered all his questions, and was regretful that there was no bar available for anyone's patronage on the premises.

After ten minutes of this surreal dialogue, the visitor ambled out the gates, and I again handed over my papers. "Ah. You want the Great Mausoleum. Drive up the hill, bear right, and there will be a person there who can direct you. Here is my card; please let me know if we may be of assistance."

I tucked his card next to its cousin and followed his instructions to an imposing structure that looked, as it was supposed to, as though it belonged in an Italian city of an earlier century. The Great Mausoleum, inspired by the Campo Santo in Genoa, Italy, was finished in 1920. I doubt any cemetery business in America today could now afford to build such a large and elaborately detailed structure. Passing through its archway, I found two older men engaged in a friendly chat, one of them bearing a multicolored bouquet. For a third time, I presented the slightly musty papers. This time the documents provoked frowns and great thoughtfulness. If the men had possessed beards, they would have been pulling on them.

"Lyman . . . Lyman . . . I know that name. Don't know where it is, though," said the man seated in the booth.

"The problem is that this gives the number of the room she's in, but we only know them now by name." He smiled ruefully, waving a hand to his friend. "Follow him, he knows where everyone is here."

David Eastburn, who, as it turned out, had no official connection with Forest Lawn, but apparently had family interred there and spent much of his free time volunteering as a decorator for services, was slightly taller and older than I, genial, and intrigued with the challenge. We roamed up and down the corridors, poking through ornate little waist-high metal gates to read the names inscribed on the walls of the private sanctuaries, which were available for visitation only to relatives of the deceased, surviving family members being referred to on signs as "property owners." We passed Clark Gable's place of honor, as well as that of William Mulholland and those of other dignitaries whose names I failed to remember or write down, so busy was I gawking at the surroundings.

Eaton's Great Mausoleum, I will be the first to admit, is an impressive environment. We passed the stained-glass reproduction of Leonardo da Vinci's *Last Supper*, the curtains that mask it having parted, as they do every hour, to the accompaniment of music and a stentorian narration. People sat in folding chairs before the sight, transfixed by this revelation. The Eaton family remains were closeted in a tasteful room to one side.

The light in the maze of corridors was dense and cool, reflecting dully off the gray-and-white marble walls and floors. The sculptures, the stained-glass windows, and the otherworldly cleanliness of the building testified to the success of Eaton's vision. The people of Forest Lawn are serious about providing service for all eternity in the style to which their patrons had become accustomed. In 1917, Eaton declared that his institutional goal was to protect the park with a perpetual endowment, ensuring that his Garden of Memory allow for the suspension of time indefinitely.

This immemorial dedication was, however, not helping us find Great-Grandmother Lyman. The last census was taken back in 1995, but approximately twenty thousand of the park's total of four hundred thousand interments are housed in the

Great Mausoleum, stacked in rows on, by my count, eight
floors and five intermediary levels that go both up and down
from the main floor. The complex is so extensive that inter-
coms are located in its more remote reaches. "To leave building,
push this button, and attendant will direct you," read the labels
affixed next to them.

Back to the front desk and a consultation, both men pag-
ing through a thick binder stuffed with floor plans that looked
like something Saint Peter would keep handy at the Gates of
Heaven.

Fingers ran down page after page, slowed, stopped. The two
men looked at each other, then at me. "Here it is. She's in the
Sanctuary of Benediction, the fanciest room in the whole place.
I think she's next to Jean Harlow. No wonder the name sounded
familiar."

Eastburn was beside himself. "What did you say your family did?"

"They were just businesspeople. Manufacturing. Coal mines
in West Virginia. Farms in Canada."

"Manufacturing what?"

"Things like leather gloves. Nothing special." I knew it was a
less-than-spectacular answer, but it also seemed appropriate for
me to deflate the situation slightly, which I felt to be escalating
far beyond my expectations. I was, in fact, feeling guilty. Here
I was, all prepared to investigate the brute parallels between
landfills and cemeteries, and I was being seduced into admi-
ration for the latter by an expensive theme park. I realized I
was also feeling less than properly respectful, dressed in baggy
cotton pants and a pullover, their saving grace being only that
they were both black.

With Eastburn leading the way, we retraced our path only a

short distance to the sanctuary, a long room with a stained-glass window at the end. He showed me how to operate the recessed button that opened the gate. "You're welcome here anytime, Mr. Fox. You don't have to tell anyone you're coming, or speak to anyone, just come whenever you like."

We entered and walked slowly into the marble hallway, a half dozen large crypts, each with its own individual gates, to either side of us. "Lyman" was next to last on the left, indeed next to Jean Harlow. Irving Thalberg, who ran MGM with Louis B. Mayer, was there. So were Pantages and Grauman, the movie theater impresarios, and the comic Red Skelton. Eastburn rattled off all the names and their pedigrees. Inside the Lyman crypt were two double marble sarcophagi with room for two more. Fresh white flowers were in a large stone urn to the right, a bench on the left. He pointed out to me that, unlike the other rooms, all of which sported pale stained-glass ceilings, the Lyman one was colored a deep blue, which perpetuated a somewhat more somber interior. In light of Eaton's design philosophy, which focused on the less moody aspects of memorialization, I doubted that the entrepreneur would have approved, though Elizabeth Lyman died in 1952 and Eaton in 1966. Apparently, she met the property owners' covenants.

"You know, you're the first person I can think of who's ever come to visit the family property, and I've been here for years and years. I'm so glad you came!"

Eastburn shook my hand and left me to my own devices, which consisted of a pen and a piece of folded notepaper, as he bustled off to place his bouquet prior to the arrival of some guests. We had taken so long to find the family crypt that I had become worried the flowers would wilt.

I sat on the surprisingly warm marble bench in the crypt

and contemplated how all my presuppositions for the day had been upset in a most interesting fashion. The paper I'd been clutching in my hand was an authorization made in 1936 by my great-grandmother and grandmother, and witnessed by my mother, to disinter William Henry Lyman Senior and Junior, my great-grandfather and grandfather, from their resting places elsewhere on the premises and to reinter them in these twin doubles of the newly purchased crypt. Great-Grandmother knew how to live it up.

When my father died, he was cremated by his second wife and there was no funeral for me to attend, nor did I particularly care. When my stepfather passed away, he, too, was cremated, his ashes placed behind a small plaque in a columbarium on a hill overlooking Reno, a building into which I've only set foot once. When Mom died, and in accordance with her wishes, I had her cremated and put the box of her "ashes"—in reality, the several pounds of bone fragments typically referred to in the business as *cremains*—in my car. I drove around with the ashes in the trunk for a month while I talked over the state of my life with her before hiking up to and scattering the remains on top of the 10,775-foot summit of Mount Rose, the tallest peak that overlooks Reno, as well as Lake Tahoe. It was a vantage point from which she could view both her house in Reno and the place she'd once had at Glenbrook on the east shore of the lake.

Perhaps she hadn't meant for me to keep her in the trunk for so long, but the point was that burial rituals in my family were pretty casual, all of us being either lapsed Presbyterians or outright atheists. The only vestigial trace of religion my mother carried in her adult life was a fondness for Celtic mysticism, and it's entirely within both her character and mine that the only reason I would have had to visit Forest Lawn would be for the sake of writing a book. Otherwise, I might never have bothered. She certainly hadn't, at least within my memory.

Why, I now asked myself, didn't she want her remains to be put with the rest of the family? She could have afforded it, but had never even brought me to pay our respects. She never mentioned how grand were the surroundings, though she had often recounted to me with pride my great-grandmother's art collection and library. If my mother hadn't left me the papers in her strongbox, the one I keep beneath my desk, and carefully written on the envelope containing them that these papers were to be kept, I would never have known.

But what created the strongest sense of wonder and puzzlement in me was the white floral arrangement, a handsome clutch of what I guessed were zinnias, and which gave off no scent that I could detect. It seemed so extravagant, flowers put where no one would see them, the wilting ones apparently replaced every week with fresh blooms. What did this say about my family's expectations of time, this conventional metaphor of the transitory counterpoised against the eternal?

After a while, I let myself out through the waist-high bronze gates, thinking that I would have to bring my two sons here. At the entrance, the friendly concierge shook my hand, said he was glad to see me—and by the way, what was it again, exactly, that my family did? "Manufacturing," I said, nodding my head.

What originally had struck me the week before from the road on Mount Lee, and from which, I now realized, I could also have seen the Forest Lawn–Glendale park, as well as the Hollywood site, was the conjunction of a cemetery with a landfill. As I drove up to the top of the memorial park, winding my way among the evergreens and outdoor courtyards with their multiple plaques and marble statuary, I couldn't help but feel as if I were traversing an elaborately designed golf course, which was the only other use of such expansive lawns that I would customarily pass in the region. Although it is much larger than the three-hundred-plus acres of Forest Lawn, the real estate value of Griffith Park, which was once valued at $1 per acre, was estimated in the late 1990s to be about $2 billion. It receives about ten million visitors annually, which seems a fair return on the dollar in public benefit, but when touring the Great Mausoleum, I'd been the only civilian in the place. Zigzagging up the hill, I saw only a half dozen other cars, which brought to mind the impossible calculus of trying to estimate the economic value of the memorial park. Presumably, a public official with an entrepreneurial genius equal to that of Eaton would be able to convert a cemetery property, once it had outlasted its usefulness as such (that is, when it was full and, like a landfill, ready to be closed), into a public park instead of a private one.

From the top of the hill where I parked and got out to walk around in the sunshine, I could see that a storm was building in the San Gabriels but that it hadn't reached Mount Wilson yet. The antennae at the summit were still clearly visible, foregrounded in the afternoon sun against the dark thunderclouds. In Great-Grandmother's day, it would have been a much cleaner ridgeline than now. In the opposite direction, I could see Mount Lee and Griffith Park. Oil money, I thought. And Hollywood money. Those are what built such an opulent necropolis. If it didn't have the scale and grandeur of the funerary complex of Karnak—the Egyptian city of the dead that stretched out over two hundred square acres and, even now, some five thousand years later, can still reduce visitors to speechlessness with the largest aggregation of funerary architecture in the world—if Forest Lawn didn't display hubris on a scale quite that monumental, it nonetheless offered up substantial evidence for the human need to elide time.

Nowadays, we are living a different kind of escape from the temporal. No longer do we think of a cemetery as a sleeping gallery where we rest momentarily before being summoned to the Pearly Gates, Saint Peter thumbing through his own version of the binder in the Great Mausoleum below to assign us to our rightful place, one earned through hard work and good deeds. Now we hardly visit the dead at all, and we leave the process of passing to the professionals. Well into the first half of the twentieth century, when a person died, it was usually at home and he or she was laid out in the living room for the wake, then carted off to the cemetery, where the body was lowered into the ground with the help of strong family arms. Fresh flowers were brought to the grave on weekends and holidays, where families often gathered for memorial picnics.

Now, we will most likely die in a hospital or another care facility. Our bodies will be whisked away by staff from the local branch of a national mortuary conglomerate, and although there may be a memorial service for us, that's not a sure thing. Our remains, which more and more these days are likely to be cremains, will be placed in the ground or in a wall or will be scattered by a family member. And that's that. Cemeteries have been relegated to the status of a specialized kind of landfill rather than a site in which the dead are said to rest, or one in which we contemplate our own mortality.

Death itself has become something that we mostly don't think about on a personal level unless it's brought forcibly to our attention by the demise of someone close to us, and even then, it's such a mediated experience that we do not remain involved with it. We don't contemplate it, which is part of a larger issue: that of how our relationship with time has changed along with our perception of space. Los Angeles well embodies the trend. Movies, and especially television, follow in the footsteps of photography, which, as the French cultural critic and architect Paul Virilio once pointed out, is a medium devoted to the "suppression of duration for the exclusive profit of the instant." Television broadcasts, he continued, were composed of "pseudo time," and he could as well have been speaking of movies. If, when visiting the modest summit of Green Mountain and looking down at the Pacific Ocean, I was standing at the terminus of Manifest Destiny, that historical force projected westward across global space, then perhaps when on Mount Wilson, I was standing at a key site in a parallel movement to colonize time.

The measurement of time, the empirical versus the experiential variety—or as Newton put it, absolute time versus relative or apparent time—has gotten so accurate that the newest clock at the National Institute of Standards and Technology (NIST) in Maryland, an "atomic fountain" device, is now off less than one second in every twenty million years. This precision has enabled scientists to define a meter no longer by the distance between scratches on a platinum bar, which is prone to changing its dimensions as the ambient temperature rises and falls, but by the distance a laser beam travels in one 299,792,458th of a second. This is the same clock against which the global positioning system is calibrated. The GPS allows a person with a handheld device to establish his or her position through the triangulation of four or more of the system's twenty-four orbiting satellites, an astonishing feat of technology. NIST is already working on an even more accurate timepiece.

Distance has been collapsed completely into time. It didn't used to be so; for centuries, time was measured in terms of the speed of the earth's rotation. Not only are we culturally wed to the diurnal cycle of light, but we're also linked irrevocably to it biologically. In 1729, an astronomer potted a heliotrope plant in a completely dark room, noting that its leaves still unfolded with the invisible rising of the sun and that they folded up again with the unseen night. This simple experiment culminated in the late 1990s with research by genetic scientists who established that specific proteins are produced in human brains and other organs on a twenty-four-hour cycle, a biomechanical clock based on genes that may have developed as early as 3.5 billion years ago.

Jonathan Weiner, who traced the research in one of his typically splendid books, *Time, Love, Memory,* noted that early organisms needed such clocks to maximize their growth, making the compounds for photosynthesis prior to the rising of the sun, and shutting down production before sunset, the schedule still followed by plants. He also pointed out that humans evolved in an African climate, where afternoon naps were an evolved adaptation to escape heat, and that violating our internal clocks may pose unknown hazards to health and sanity. Human beings followed the diurnal cycle until only very recently, the natural rhythms abrogated only with two linked innovations: the widespread use of artificial light and the adoption of a global time scheme.

It wasn't until the Prime Meridian Conference held in 1884 that a single location, Greenwich, England, became the place where midnight was set for the world, and its opposite, the antemeridian, was established as the international date line. Time, which before then was set locally by the advent of noon, was finally standardized worldwide. Once a common prime meridian was accepted—a convention necessitated by the increasing speed of railway trains and passenger ships, which took more and more passengers across multiple time zones—the effort to measure time more accurately accelerated to keep up with the effects of technology. The more accurate clocks then allowed for the manufacturing of machines and instruments with higher tolerances for stress, which led to the development of airplanes and air travel, which in turn required clocks even more accurate for navigation. To say that time and space are entwined in a technological synergy is to state the obvious.

The speed of the earth changes every year; the gravity of the moon (expressed as tidal friction) and the varying strengths of monsoonal winds pushing against the Himalaya each year slow down the globe. The water impounded behind dams in the Northern Hemisphere acts as a flywheel and slows the rate of slowing. These and other factors necessitate the adding of a leap-second every few years, which is close enough for figuring out when to plant your crops. But for the transmission of data in wavelengths packed so closely together on Mount Wilson that the differences must be measured in nanoseconds, or billionths of a second, lest they overlap and the electromagnetic signals become pure garble, the measurement of time needs to be more precise.

The official national time of the nation has been broadcast on radio by the NIST since 1923. After World War II, research conducted on radar and extremely high-frequency radio transmissions made possible the application of microwaves to research in physics—those same emissions that my father was studying in the North Atlantic and that now pour off the towers atop

Mount Wilson. With this new capability, scientists had the leisure to beam microwaves at various atoms, discovering that
they could thus measure the vibrations of atoms, which had a
very constant oscillation indeed. The first atomic clock came
into use by NIST in 1949 and was calibrated to the oscillations
of ammonia atoms. Every Sunday, my father would arise, tune
in to WWV, the NIST station then and now, and reset the clocks
of the house according to its signal. He was so strict about this
ritual that he once slapped me for attempting to put the clocks
forward to the correct time after a power outage on a weekend
morning. I had happened to arise before him and thought I was
performing a helpful ritual, but his rage for control after experiencing the chaos of war had forever diminished his capacity
to tolerate what he perceived as pedestrian meddling with the
order of the universe.

Unfortunately, we have no device like an atomic clock by
which we can plot the present along our individual timelines.
We have no way of measuring experiential time except through
sequence and memory, although we do understand that one
thing follows another, a pragmatic approach rooted in, oddly
but most naturally, the second law of thermodynamics. For-
mulated by the German physicist Rudolf Clausius in 1859, the
law states that heat cannot flow, by itself, from a cooler to a
hotter body. Heat in one place will always flow to a place where
less heat is present, until the temperature of the two spots is in
equilibrium. Similarly, molecules and physical momentum will
always move from an area of higher concentration to one of
lower concentration. This observation doesn't seem like such a
blinding insight when you're watching the teakettle on the stove
as it cools to room temperature, but when the law is applied on
the cosmological level, it's stunning.

Here's a classic example of the implications. Open a perfume bottle, and leave it unstoppered for a few days. The perfume evaporates, of course, into thin air — or, to be more precise, the atmosphere of the room. You may have noticed the scent when walking into the room, although if the door of the room has been open to the rest of the house, the scent has so dispersed you wouldn't be able to perceive it, even with that vaunted perceptual ability to distinguish those ten thousand smells that can trigger memories in the limbic system. The molecules of perfume have exercised the universal trait of all things to mix with one another, given enough time.

Can you imagine that the perfume might actually flow back into the bottle all by itself? No. The reason is that the second law of thermodynamics cannot be reversed; the molecules aren't going to line up and march back into the bottle. There isn't enough time in the theoretical life span of the universe for that infinitely small probability to be exercised. You also know this fact intuitively (without having to be shown the mathematics or performing any number of experiments) as well as from simple experience: The pieces of a broken cup do not fall upward and reassemble themselves on the table. That is, the highly ordered, dense structure of the original cup has "flowed" to the more chaotic, more dispersed broken shards.

This irreversibility, the unidirectional procession of events, is what physicists call *time's arrow.* On a cosmic scale, this means that energy radiates out from the sun and every other star and dissipates, some of the energy reaching Mount Wilson and other observatories as photons — and the photons aren't going to march backward to the stars. This thermodynamic property is the universe winding down, its heat running into the cold, all the universe ending up the same even temperature of absolute zero (minus 459.72°F). The second law of thermodynamics also means, literally, that all the information in the universe will end up in the same state, since information is also subject to this law of nature. Information is merely news of difference, as I previously paraphrased the anthropologist Gregory Bateson; the corollary is that all difference seeks to equalize.

Movies comprise duration and sequence, and given the ubiquity of such entertainment in our lives, the way that filmmakers and television writers engineer time is bound to influence our perception of its nature. Today, we have bred in us an impatience for any problem not resolved within an hour or two, and the assumption that death is irrelevant.

All but the most abstract, avant-garde films are based on story. Stories organize information into linear narratives to explain, or at least pretend to explain, how the world works. We are never so pleased as when, watching a romantic comedy, we find that an apparent coincidence in the beginning turns out to be the singular device causing the protagonists to meet and fall in love. We very much want the world to be tidied up into narratives that demonstrate increasing order, where everything has meaning that progresses to higher and higher states of being (love, discovery, enlightenment).

And, of course, those things happen constantly in life—but in any universal scheme of things, they are only momentary stays against entropy, or the ever-increasing disorder of the universe, the numbing and progressive loss of information that we call death. Ashes to ashes, dirt to dirt, as it were.

Watching the movie *Volcano* encourages us to believe that we can create order out of disorder. And it is possible. If we redirect enough energy from one place to another, we can counter the entropy for a bit. As John McPhee points out in his book

The Control of Nature, which contains an essay about chan-
neling catastrophic lava flows in Iceland, such efforts succeed
only momentarily. That's the same book that describes how the
San Gabriels are busy falling down all over the northern edge
of the Los Angeles Basin, much to the eternal frustration of
those engineers who work in that division of city government
referred to as Flood. The mountains are obeying the second
law of thermodynamics, the heights merely seeking equilibrium with the basin below. And Great-Grandmother? With her
efforts to make a perpetual monument to the dead, is she any
different from the engineers who strive to fight the erosion of
mountains?

All these fights against time are writ large in the City of Angels.
Volcano is a twentieth-century rendering of the nineteenth-
century painting of Vesuvius made into a spectacle of grand
proportions—but whereas the painting shows nature truly
beyond our control, the citizens in the movie band together
and defeat nature. People living around the La Brea Tar Pits
believe that we have the methane likewise under control. Only
when the cracks in the middle of the streets every now and then
burst into flame do we worry, the threat otherwise out of sight
and, therefore, mind.

From atop every ridge around the basin, and increasingly
from every tall structure in the city, we broadcast microwaves
in an attempt to make simultaneous every desire and wish and
want and need, and to match them with information, a solution,
a fix, a purchase. The information superhighway is in virtual
parallel with the freeways. Given L.A.'s size and geographical
dispersion, distance from point to point is measured by most
people not in the number of miles, but in driving time. "Everything is either twenty or forty-five minutes away," Angelenos

commonly say. We can't compress the physical space, so we attempt to shorten the time, hence the original rationale for the freeways.

The average speed on freeways in Los Angeles County is now about that of an average four-lane boulevard, a handy enough simile for the frustrations we experience with cruising the Internet. In terms of information, we're seeking to eliminate the telephone wires and television cables that constrict our instant access to the world, and go wireless. We won't just be broadcasting information anymore, but raw data in unimaginable quantities that will be measured, again, by time, in this case the intervals it takes to download the data.

And as for our final and inescapable inability to escape the temporal? We divorce ourselves from having to handle the evidence of those who pass away before we do. If we can no longer afford to build enormous and elaborate Romanesque mausoleums in the middle of town, or purchase marble rooms endowed with weekly cut flowers to show that we have bought ourselves an endless living memory, then we take the next step. We go virtual. For a few thousand dollars, cemeteries in Los Angeles, and increasingly elsewhere, will edit the photographic images of your life into a DVD or another digital storage device of your choice. And there, in front of whoever is left and will care to watch, will be your eternal image prancing as a child through the sprinklers on a hot summer's afternoon, your march to the altar on your wedding day, and the birth of your children. You will have become the star of your own movie.

We love those endings that wrap up the world for us, whether it's a compelling historical documentary that leads us to believe we understand what caused a world war, or a romance movie where the lovers get married because events showed them to be destined for each other. A digital record of Grandfather's life we can show the kids provides the same kind of narrative logic, as if to say, "This is where I came from, and you, too."

Well, at least for a little while. Until the information decays on the plastic, escaping into thin air as surely as will all the perfume in the world—given time. The idea that we would attempt to elevate ourselves into coherent narratives suitable for immortality makes for good irony against the experience of those citizens who had never before seen the Milky Way and panicked during the blackout when it blazed across the sky for the first time in memory. It's as if, lacking the stars of the night sky, we had to invent our own—as if, lacking an awareness of the geological time beneath our feet and the cosmic clock wheeling above us, we had to invent some other kind of extrahuman timescale.

A human being can't perceive two events as separate unless they occur more than thirty milliseconds apart. (A common household camera can stop action down to a single millisecond, or one thousandth of a second, at which virtually all human motion appears to be frozen.) Even our ears, which have many times more nerve endings than our visual system and which are exquisitely able to distinguish microtonal intervals in music, can't separate phonemes if they occur more quickly than thirty milliseconds. Speech simply becomes unintelligible noise. Nor are we any good at holding in mind a perception longer than a few seconds. Present a person with one of those ambiguous drawings, such as the black-and-white outline that looks like either two profiles facing each other or the outline of a vase, and the mind flips back and forth between the two versions every three seconds, as if to query the world for news of change. Of difference.

We have memory, which allows us to move beyond this rapid scanning of the environment and to create sequence out of it. Memory enables us to retain knowledge of how to survive and how to use tools—including the written word—and to pass knowledge from generation to generation and to hold a story in mind. Memory, although it is rooted in the limbic system, essentially the part of the brain that dates back to when we were all reptiles, is an ability that seems to have exploded concurrent with the expansion of the forebrain, the *neocortex,* which occurred when mammals arose on the planet 220 million years ago. Jonathan Weiner points out, however, that the genes responsible for rudimentary memory may be as old as those producing in us a sense of time.

Think of what an advantage memory is. Without memory, you would have to rely solely on either direct, real-time response to stimuli—a response such as running away from a predator when it appeared in front of you—or genetically encoded information. For example, you might avoid a certain smell instinctively, since you knew that it meant a predator had passed by recently. But with memory, you can remember consciously where you have seen a predator before, and thus avoid crossing its path in the future. Further, imagine how powerful a survival skill for hominids was the ability to remember a story told to you by someone else years ago about how to kill the predator with nothing more than a sharp stick when it attacked you.

Our desire to link events in a linear fashion stems from an ancient and extensive set of survival traits, indeed ones that powerfully compel us toward story, which is a ubiquitous way of organizing memory. Story is, however, an artifice. It's subject to every kind of tinkering we can invent in books and movies, and we sometimes run the risk of losing memory for the sake of compressing a story in time.

An attempt to colonize time has been added to our preoccupation with achieving Manifest Destiny in space. If we have run out of uncharted planetary surface over which to extend our graticule of cartography, our presumed ruler, hence the illusion of rule, then we will reach back in time for an energy source allowing us to condense the present and move ever more quickly into the future. We plunder ancient reservoirs of oil, as we do fossil water in underground aquifers, and ignore the fact that both are limited resources that will run out. We heat the water to make electricity, use more water to cool off the power plant . . . and the power we generate goes straight into the telecommunications network that we use to eliminate gaps in time and space.

This synergy seems like merely a literary trope, so tight is the loop, but in the spring of 2001, when the first of the rolling blackouts fell across California, it was all too obvious that this cycle was also a fact. Less visible was how the increasing colonization of the electromagnetic spectrum, and the concomitant compression of media production with digital technology, would pollute our sense of time, producing other kinds of sensory blackouts. Forecasting technological advances in our ability to compress time—and stories—is increasingly a risky business, given the constant evolution of the tools involved, but some changes are very nearly here.

What does it mean when you can take a script and film it with handheld digital camcorders over a few weeks, not months, and edit the results in days instead of weeks? And then telephone the resulting movie to theaters across the country in seconds? Better yet, pipe the results directly into wireless household digital TVs. Translating a concept in a writer's mind to that of the audience might not take several years, or even several months, but might soon occur within a few days. Imagine movies made as fast and cheaply as soap operas. Think of the films' disappearing from the collective consciousness just as quickly. Think of India's hyperprolific Bollywood, which cranks out dozens of movies per week, eight hundred a year, compared with just over a hundred by Hollywood. Imagine an audience able to download the new version of any story to fit any mood all the time. These are changes that are already here. Think of how reality will compete.

Well, of course, reality doesn't compete with anything. No disaster movie will prevent an earthquake, a flood, or even a divorce. Imagine our puzzlement when, having allowed our cognitive triage to remove all memory of such events, the roof comes crashing down on our heads in a violent rainstorm while we're eating dinner in front of the television.

Or such, anyway, was the vision I had as I drove back down the steep, winding drive of Forest Lawn, realizing as I did so that the hilltop of the cemetery would be a perfect site for a cluster of cell-phone towers. Perhaps they could be disguised as large replicas of Michelangelo's *David*.

We consider time both linear and cyclical. It goes forward, inexorably, but it also circles back around, the rotation of the planet and the solar system and the galaxy all great wheels in space exhibiting periodicity to which life has adapted with great specificity in its genetic code. Just as we have cultivated the ability to cover great distances and modify the space around us from the atomic level up to the scale of global climate, so we are slowly learning to transform if not time's absolute arrow, at least our experience of it. We lose touch with the ground we walk on and the Milky Way. We camouflage the process of aging and distance ourselves from death and fill the electromagnetic spectrum with our voices in an effort to do so.

We collapse the linearity of time inasmuch as we try to make everything happen simultaneously. We trivialize its cycles down to a new season of television shows and reminders from Hallmark, in September, that it's time to buy Christmas cards.

I drove slowly out the gate in late afternoon. The attendant in his booth was pressing materials promoting pre-need solutions into the hands of a bewildered young couple who looked as if they were looking for nothing more than a quiet corner to themselves for a few minutes before closing time. As I headed home, I was thinking that schools should organize field trips not just to the La Brea Tar Pits and the observatories on Mount Wilson, but also to the RF jungle and local cemeteries.

It's not as if we're going to stop the colonization of time any more than the Luddites were able to shut down the increasingly mechanized textile mills of England in the early nineteenth century. Short-term increases in consumer convenience and cost savings, which produce powerful profit incentives to businesses, usually outweigh long-term dangers to social structure and health as factors in public-policy decision making. The spread of wireless communications among cell phones, computers, and other electronic devices is the case in point, and our presence throughout the airwaves will continue to spread as we seek to communicate absolutely everything wirelessly, point to every pinpoint on the planet. To say that we're going to be increasingly distracted away from the world by its electronic twin, an environment in which we routinely bend time to our individual needs and corporate efficiencies, is merely to extend what's already happening.

To keep ourselves anchored to the natural world, we're going to have to walk around in human-designed places that ignore nature, not just places set aside to celebrate nature or where placards tells us we're supposed to pay attention to scenic climax. The nonurban character of Yosemite National Park, which each year hosts a visiting population the size of L.A.'s, is only half the picture. We need to look at the nature we're piping underground to refineries, broadcasting from ridgetops, and putting into landfills, the latter an archeological realm that hosts Great-Grandmother's trash as well as last week's newspapers. This is the environment we are creating—not a more natural infrastructure of forests and lakes and plains from which we derive food, planks for shelter, and fiber for clothing, but a less natural network of pipes and wires, tunnels and towers. This is a part of the world we also have to understand in order to retain a sense of time and our collective memory.

We need to take such walks more than once, in fact at regular intervals, so we can see for ourselves the changes we are making. And maybe it's not such a bad thing to track some tar into the house from the La Brea Tar Pits, after all.

in the meantime

I started writing the first of these essays in late 1999, finished the third one in mid-2001, and then set them aside for travel and work on other projects. I returned to Los Angeles in 2003 and resumed work on *Making Time*, in the process moving from past to present tense in the essays. Enough had changed in the intervening months that some updates are also in order.

The new shopping center by Park La Brea, the Grove, has become one of the most popular shopping destinations in Los Angeles, and the number of apartments built around the older planned community has almost doubled. The blocks in between Fairfax Street and La Brea Avenue, with Third Street on the north and Wilshire Boulevard on the south, are now one of the densest urban areas in America. The new buildings vent the ubiquitous methane through tall standpipes and maintain sensitive monitors to detect interior leaks. A visitor can see the instruments on the pillars of the parking structures. The nearby museums have enclosed the seeps of tar in their parking lots with chain-link cages and have torn down the elevated platform from which tourists used to pitch their lit cigarettes at the natural-gas bubbles in the tar pits, which should be of some consolation to the visiting schoolteachers and their charges.

Skyrocketing land values during 2003–2005 led to the abandonment of an increasing number of oil wells across the basin in favor of housing developments and strip malls. In March 2004, an orphaned well in Huntington Beach blew out in a gusher forty feet high, spraying oil and methane over one-half square mile, a hazardous-waste problem that will become more common. On the other hand, the price of oil rose past seventy dollars a barrel just as the housing market began to cool, and a few wells were reopened.

The Belmont Learning Center, now designated the Central Los Angeles High School No. 11/Vista Hermosa Park, was still unoccupied, but, with some modifications, is expected to open in the future. The school district will soon tear down two existing buildings and relocate their functions into new ones, then mitigate the methane and hydrocarbon problems by venting, installing a series of gas barriers under the foundations, and sealing the utilities in trenches. The portions of the property for which venting might be insufficient will be used as open parkland.

In July 2002, a team of FCC inspectors visited the telecommunications facilities on Mount Wilson and found that a person could approach most of the antennae without facing fences or even warning signs about radio frequency radiation. Several fines were levied. By 2005, the number of U.S. cell towers that stood between 90 and 200 feet high had grown to more than 170,000; added to towers that imitated pine trees and saguaro were models made to resemble oak trees and magnolias.

In 2003, the Cremation Association of North America projected that cremations would rise from 27 percent of all deaths in 2001 to 36 percent in 2010 and then 44 percent in 2025, a rate rising faster than the increases in mortality projected for the same period. In 2005, the upper reaches of both the Hollywood Hills branch of Forest Lawn Memorial Parks and the Mount Sinai Memorial Parks looked like subdivisions under development. Their new terraces were being graded in anticipation of new residences needed for the baby boomers, who that year officially started to retire and were creating a housing bubble entirely different from the one their children were creating.

As for me, having escaped the increasing upward mobility and rents of the Mid-Wilshire District in Los Angeles, I'm now living in the Rancho Equestrian neighborhood of Burbank, the southeastern corner of the old Rancho Providencia that abuts Griffith Park and the Los Angeles Equestrian Center. I can walk a few blocks, pass under a freeway through a pedestrian culvert, and find myself on the edge of the Los Angeles River. Once across a bridge, I enter more than two hundred miles of roads, trails, and unmarked paths that lead upward to wander the ridges in between the two cities.

It would be a mistake to think of Burbank as a bucolic setting. But in the morning, a flock of small, wild, green parrots hangs upside down eating the fruit on the silk tree next door. The parrots—which like the tree are originally from the rain forests of South America—are just one of the thirty-three feral parrot species found in the L.A. region, most of them escaped importees. In the evenings, mallard ducks fly overhead from the river, where they've been swimming among the willows. And in the still hours of the night, I'm more likely to be wakened by the horses that surround our house on three sides than by the helicopters that haunt L.A. The ground booms softly as the horses stamp their feet at the neighborhood raccoons, coyotes, opossum, and skunks that wander about. It's easy to forget momentarily that within a few blocks in any direction is a freeway, and that the smog levels in the summer are the worst in the nation.

The measurement of time continues to be refined. In July 2001, British researchers had surpassed the NIST standard of cesium atom accuracy (the NIST clock losing one second every twenty million years) by measuring the much-higher-frequency optical oscillations of a single ion of mercury (1.064 quadrillion ticks per second). The projected loss of time by the clock was pared to a second per hundred million years. Because this refinement will greatly increase the accuracy of the global positioning system, the new British clock has excited the geologists who spend their careers measuring how fast continents move, as well as aerospace engineers at NASA plotting trajectories to Mars. It is perhaps a little less meaningful to Los Angeleno commuters, who now spend an average of 136 hours per year stuck on the freeways during the rush hour, which lasts from approximately 6–10 AM to 4–7 PM.

The Brits are hoping to get their future clocks down to losing only a second per ten billion years. But first they have to revise how a second is defined, since the new accuracy applied over such time lengths based on the old seconds would lead to a hopeless mess, yet another gridlock in space and time.

THE PRESENT PERFECT CONTINUOUS

Walking up the dirt access road on the northeast side of the ninety-acre Toyon Landfill is a slow process, the steep grade more suited to bulldozers than hikers. But the hike has been worth it this spring, the landfill thigh-deep in wildflowers until the last couple of weeks, when unseasonably hot weather began to burn back the grasses and perennials to a tawny mixture of tans, golds, and browns. The mountain lion that has been living here for what may have been at least a year and a half cannot be seen in such terrain unless it moves almost directly across your field of vision, so well adapted is its coloration to the sun-burnt biota of Southern California.

When I reach the top of the hill, I have two options. To my left a dirt road cuts up to follow one of the dozen terraces sculpted into the face of the landfill, a path favored by most of the horseback riders up here. The other route goes straight and around the top of the landfill to meet up with the paved but long-closed Mount Hollywood Drive, the choice of bicycle riders and most hikers accessing the northeast quadrant of Griffith Park. I opt for the latter in order to wind my way up to Mount Bell, one of the small summits east of Mount Lee. I'll then return on the bridle path, a circuit that will afford me a variety of views over Burbank and the rest of the San Fernando Valley.

The park is often labeled somewhat incongruously "America's largest urban wilderness." Its 4,212 acres of chaparral and pockets of forest are home to mammals ranging from mice and squirrels to the mountain lion—but, in addition to the landfill, the park contains a golf course, a zoo, and, directly in front of me, the nine-megawatt electrical generating station that runs off the gas generated by the decomposing waste in the landfill. The electric plant's chugging generators put out enough power to light up forty-five hundred homes, and I'm glad to move out of earshot when I enter the trees on the other side of the artificial plateau.

As I am wont to do when moving to a new location, I seek the high ground for orientation. I've taken to walking up the northeastern corner of the park, near the terminus of the Hollywood Hills. Just as the hills offer fine views of the Los Angeles Basin from their other side, from here they provide me with some easily accessed aerial perspective on the San Fernando Valley, much of which was scraped flat and filled with subdivisions after World War II. The valley also happens to be the home of major media corporations, such as Disney, ABC, and NBC. The conjunction of city, film, and nature is much on my mind lately, as is the history of horses in the city and in movies. I have ridden horses since I was a kid and like living among them. I can't help but admire them as a species well suited to my meditations on time and how we attempt to reconfigure it to fit our purposes.

Once you are past the open slopes, a lush oak woodland embraces the road. A Nuttall's Woodpecker hammers briskly away at an oak trunk until it sees me, then shyly inches around the tree to hide until I pass. The park's dense foliage is host to a good portion of the city's estimated five thousand coyotes and numerous deer, the latter being the favored food of the mountain lion. A half dozen or so of these pumas live in the Santa Monica Mountains between here and the Pacific Coast, where the range ends roughly forty miles to the west. Between four thousand and six thousand of the cats live in the state, and where they have free range, an average of five to seven animals can occupy 100 square miles. It's not surprising to find a puma almost anywhere in the hills of Southern California—but it took the rangers aback a week before my walk to find one bedding down in a park that is not much more than 5 square miles in extent and that sees upward of ten million visitors a year. A full-grown male puma, which can attain two hundred pounds and from tip of nose to tail can measure eight feet long, requires a hunting ground of up to 150 square miles. How the cat will survive here is a bit of a puzzle that involves the puma's ability to connect the park with other regional habitats.

The local equestrians had first reported the presence of a big cat in the park, accounts that the rangers initially disbelieved. Horses don't like pumas and get skittish around their scent, and riders have a higher vantage point than hikers do and can thus spot other animals more easily. Plus, if you're on horseback, you don't have to watch your feet as the horse walks. You can look around and have an entirely different arrangement with nature than do other residents of L.A. Most of the local riders know perfectly well the differences between a German shepherd and a coyote, between a bobcat and a puma, and when they report seeing a mountain lion, it's worth a second look. Still, the rangers weren't convinced until the superintendent of the landfill saw a large cat at dusk while the man was sitting in his vehicle near the power plant. Now the rangers are hurriedly posting signs warning of the potential danger of attacks. It's an unfortunate and lopsided equation that most of the riders are women and it took the word of a man to attract the attention of officialdom. American bureaucrats, whether male or female, remain more likely to accept the authority of a woman about flowers than about charismatic megafauna.

I pause for a drink of water at a rocky outcropping that, when the road was open to public traffic, must have been a popular pullout. Below me the colonial brick buildings and Italianate statues at the Hollywood Hills branch of Forest Lawn face off with the eighty-five-foot-high, star-spangled "Sorcerer's Apprentice" hat at Disney's animation and film studios across the Los Angeles River. Holding up the horizontal pediment under the roof of one of the buildings are the Seven Dwarfs from *Snow White*—or, rather, nineteen-foot-high sculptures of the characters. The nearby ABC building stands on the site where Walt Disney planned to build the Mickey Mouse Park, precursor to what was to become the Disneyland amusement park located on a much larger property to the south in Orange County.

The scene below, a juxtaposition of fantasy themes that you'd expect more on the Las Vegas Strip than in suburban Los Angeles, alludes to the desert city's historical linkages with the motel architecture of the original strip, Hollywood's Sunset Strip. Besides sharing architects and landscape designers, the cities have a shared media culture. MGM, for example, owns about half the casinos on the Vegas Strip. Burbank is sometimes referred to—by the media—as "the media capital of the world." It's easy to scoff at such hyperbole applied to a modest city of only 100,000 or so residents and where business streets consist of block after block of single-story storefronts, auto repair shops, and fast-food outlets, a city that is sandwiched between Hollywood and the $9-billion-a-year porn industry just to the northwest, in Chatsworth. But three major studios, the West Coast offices of two of the three television networks, several major recording companies, and more than six hundred media-related businesses are located in Burbank.

Surreal juxtapositions cannot fail to abound in a place so dominated by the cinematic imagination, so media capital it is. Burbank is one of some eighty cities in Los Angeles County with a population of less than 125,000. Along with Glendale, it anchors the lower southeastern corner of the San Fernando Valley, a basin twenty by twelve miles and containing more than 1.7 million people. "The Valley," used by Steven Spielberg and other directors to represent the archetypal American suburb, is large enough to contain San Francisco; Washington, D.C.; and Boston.

The Los Angeles River runs the length of the entire valley, and the river's headwaters consolidate a few miles to my left and out of sight, where the Bell and Calabasas creeks flow out of the Santa Susanna and Santa Monica mountains, respectively, then join forces behind the bleachers of Canoga Park High School. Between there and where I live in Burbank, ten more creeks join in, all of them converted into concrete conduits, part of the county's more than 470 miles of open flood channels, a network of mysterious possibilities that commuters drive across without a thought.

By the time the river curves around the park to enter the Glendale Narrows that start a few blocks from where I live—a passage that is one of the river's few unpaved stretches—more than eighty million gallons are flowing down the river daily, most of it treated wastewater. During the heaviest rain last winter, I walked to the riverbank and marveled at waves roiling in muddy waters ten feet deep. Water swept around islands of willows and cottonwood trees with the same speed and force of a flash flood in a desert canyon. The channels are built to handle a hundred-year flood, a calculation that during my fifty-some years of living in the American Southwest I have seen revised over and over to accommodate increasingly violent weather events supposedly outside the range of statistics.

Right now the creeks are only trickling and the river is about eighteen inches deep, as these waterways would have been when the mountain lion used them to thread its way under the streets of Burbank and the maze woven by Interstate 5 and the Route 101 and 134 freeways. Naturalists theorize that the puma is probably a juvenile male forced out of its home territory by older cats and the limited hunting available in the Verdugo Mountains, the small subrange that stands between Burbank and the massive front range of the San Gabriels. Whenever I get confused about the number and orientation of the 650 miles of local freeways, I walk up onto the slopes of the mountains here to contemplate the complex folding of multiple ranges and drainages ringing the San Fernando Valley. Puma or person, you learn your way around.

After an hour of wandering up the closed roadway and then branching west on a dirt fire road, I attain the summit of Mount Bell at 1,587 feet. It's only an 800-foot ascent from my starting place below the landfill, and my route is shared with people on foot, bicycle, and horseback. But on a clear day like today, you can see from the ocean to Mount Wilson, and the entire San Fernando Valley is laid out before you in a series of interlocking grids, most of which run determinedly north to south, east to west, but abut with others that are offset by twenty or thirty or forty degrees to parallel the mountains. In fact, the eastern side of the valley, including the equestrian corner where I live, was oriented to the tracks of the Southern Pacific Railroad, which

linked San Francisco and Los Angeles in 1876. The tracks, seeking the most direct path south to Cahuenga Pass and into Los
Angeles, followed the drainage along the southern flanks of the
Verdugo Mountains. San Fernando Road and then downtown
Burbank were laid out parallel to the tracks. The Burbank grid
is thus topographically instead of cartographically fixated. Its
alignment with the dominant landform, the Verdugos, makes
perfect sense to the eye, but where it abuts the streets that run
along the cardinal directions, the grid is forced into a series of
sharp kinks—which makes absolutely no sense to the mind.

Perhaps I should be more explicit. The eye is a complex
extension of the brain, not really a separate organ in the way
that we normally think of it. And, as I mentioned earlier, we
discard most of the visual information that flows in through
that channel, lest we cook the circuitry. So every view we have
of land is a constructed landscape, every facet of nature resolved
into the two dozen or so geometric shapes that we use to parse
the world into comprehensibility. And squares and rectangles
are the kinds of simple and closed structures that the brain most
prefers. Even when geometry doesn't really exist in nature, we
tend to construe such, a tendency labeled *pareidolia.* Percival
Lowell observing canals on Mars late in the nineteenth century provides a good example. When Lowell looked at the Red
Planet through his telescope in Flagstaff, Arizona, his brain
automatically connected random natural features into straight
lines, transforming what the Italian astronomer Giovanni
Schiaparelli had said earlier might be natural canals into engi-
neered channels. Lowell then spun his visual illusion into the
public works of a Martian civilization built to hold at bay the
encroaching desert of a dying planet.

When we enter a landscape new to us, we decide automatically and usually unconsciously how it is oriented to the compass, which is not only a matter of natural magnetism in the earth, but a cultural convention reinforced for two millennia by maps. Drive around most of Los Angeles, and it appears that you're bearing along one of the four cardinal directions. For the most part, the appearance that your mind has constructed is correct. Head toward the ocean on Wilshire Boulevard or Sunset Boulevard, and you're usually heading west. Hence the name of the latter. When we enter a new space, however, we often get the orientation wrong, and we're stuck with it unless we spend what seems like an inordinate amount of time and energy recalibrating ourselves. Kinks in streets that are caused by offsets from the cardinal points of the compass radically confuse us.

The Swedish-born engineer Erik Jonsson grew up exploring the severely isotropic forests of Sweden, worked in the cities of Europe as a young man, and in the late 1960s moved to San Diego, where he has resided ever since. A wilderness hiker with a profoundly well-developed sense of direction, he nonetheless feels prey to various kinds of cognitive disorientations when traveling, many of which he recounts in his concise book, *Inner Navigation.* Jonsson traces how we develop cognitive or mental maps under a variety of circumstances; he says that we most often use both natural and man-made landmarks to first construct a "direction frame." The author then walks us through example after example of how we inadvertently disable ourselves when taking plane rides, falling asleep on trains, and simply reading maps incorrectly. If you've ever traveled to a strange city at night, gone to bed in a hotel room, and then woken up thinking the sun had risen on the wrong side of town, you'll have lived one of his stories.

Jonsson's theory is that we evolved as primates ranging

within a fairly small area, and that our ability to form a detailed cognitive map is superb for that purpose, but that once we start to wander afar, the ability is overtaxed. I grew up in Reno, where the mountains run south to north. Even though I am now living in Burbank, my internal map insists that the sun rises to the east over a ridge and sets to the west over another ridge, the most prominent landmarks visible in Reno. Here in Burbank, the sun rises in between the Verdugos and the ridge of the Santa Monicas that form Griffith Park, and then sets over what from our house appears to be a flat plain. After four months, I'm getting used to living on the diagonal, as I did at Park La Brea, but I carry a sheaf of maps in the car.

One of the most efficient ways to cope with disorientation is literally to rise above it, and all my life I've been walking up hills to get my bearings. My hike today to Mount Bell is the first time I've had a chance to get above Burbank since moving here, and it affords me a chance to look down on the abutment of Burbank's streets with the north-south grid in the rest of the valley and to visually connect it with the grid on the other side of the hills, where I lived before. I take visual bearings on Mount Wilson, the Forest Lawn facility in Glendale, then the house, weaving together both time and space, not to mention the first and second parts of this narrative, yet another kind of orientation for me, the establishment of a continuum out of disparate parts.

While I'm standing on the modest summit, a jetliner makes its final approach to the Burbank Airport. The aircraft is actually lower in altitude than I am and seems to fly at an impossibly slow speed, a common illusion caused by the mind's inability to accept how large the machine is in the air with nothing nearby for a size comparison. Without so much as a pause, the scene before me suddenly morphs into a miniature train set. The cars, like the plane, become toys. Any time we're above an observed terrain, we run the risk that the mind will attempt to establish a cohesive picture by dropping out details, oversimplifying, and falsely linking random items to one another. Pareidolia, the aforementioned tendency to construct known features in spatial dimensions from unconnected dots, can also be taken as a temporal metaphor for how we construct history from the high ground of the present. It's a literally irresistible habit, attempting to massage an episodic reality into a narrative.

I rotate around, able to scan much of the county's 16,692-mile network of city streets surrounding the park on all sides, a pattern of development that has been followed by other cities of the American West. Phoenix has swallowed any number of peaks standing in the middle of the Valley of the Sun, setting them aside as recreational areas. Las Vegas is spilling out of its valley to surround the mountain range to the south, which has been declared a conservation area. Part of the reason is that steep terrain isn't economically feasible to build on. You can construct homes on almost any slope, but not only is doing so expensive, the hillside soil is easily washed away during the intense downpours of desert precipitation. It may not rain all that much in Los Angeles, but as the brown waters in the river during the winter attest, our annual fifteen inches tend to come in severe events that saturate soils and erode entire hillsides in minutes. The same is true in the other arid cities, although in L.A., we also have earthquakes adding to the tension of living on a hillside, not to mention wildfires pushed upslope by the desert winds periodically unleashed across the basin.

A congruent reason for preserving the heights is the notion that they are territories we all share visually. They are not only our navigational landmarks in space, but also our most obvious connection to what we conceive of as having once been predeveloped and nonurban landscape; the summits are thus landmarks in time. We reinforce the economics of development with aesthetic regulations keeping houses off the ridges and with environmental codes specifying the preservation of the watershed, thus creating the visual allusion to (and illusion of) an unspoiled and healthy habitat, a relict landscape. We get above the landscape and simplify both the space below us and its historical time, and privilege the vantage to create a viewscape.

And what a view it is: Griffith Park, with its terraced landfill. The city zoo adjacent to the park and surrounded by 6½ miles of tall chain-link fence to keep the coyotes away from its twelve hundred animals, in particular the flamingos and penguins, of which the wild canines are fond. The power plant, the observatory, the golf course. The hand-lettered signs on the trails that ask people not to feed the coyotes. This is not any kind of wilderness. On the other hand, Burbank, with its parrots and ducks and blue jays, its opossums and squirrels, its barns and horses, is not pure city, either. Two blocks east from where I live, there are dirt alleyways and barnyards; head in the opposite direction, and you run into Warner Brothers and Nickelodeon. From both points, however, the equally mixed terrain of the park remains the most visible geography.

With that thought, I head back down, this time following a dozen tourists on horseback on a dusty bridle path. They've passed up over the ridge from the Los Angeles side and are headed down into Burbank for a Mexican dinner, a long-standing tradition. The riders include several middle-aged women and a young couple, the female half of which is discussing with the wrangler, a lean and slightly piratical-appearing sort, how she can obtain lessons—"Not that I want to go riding by myself, but maybe with someone visiting from out of town?" He allows that such a thing is possible, and I miss the rest of the mildly flirtatious exchange, as I'm actually walking faster than the mounted group, trying to outpace the flies that follow the equestrians.

Horses have been in North America for 50 million years, starting with the *Eohippus,* an animal the size of a terrier with legs ending in hooves instead of toes. A million years ago, horses as large as modern-day ponies were being eaten by the saber-toothed cats in the L.A. Basin, but both species went extinct around 10,000 years ago, as did most of the large mammals in North America when the last ice age ended and people were coming onto the continent in a large way. Horses apparently survived the climate changes and overhunting only in Asia, along with their cousins the zebras in Africa. Eventually, the horses were domesticated around 5000 BC. Through waves of human invasion, the horses were spread again across Europe, until the Spaniards brought them back to the New World in the 1500s, whereupon the modern-day horse began to breed on the plains as if it had never left.

The 250 or so horses that are housed in Burbank are a good example of how diverse their purposes and breeds have become. Riders in one ring at the Equestrian Center wear black velvet helmets and practice the prancing steps of dressage on thoroughbreds, while in another ring, cowboy hats signify those who run their quarter horses through the equally demanding choreography of pen racing and cutting calves. People ride on Western saddles, on English saddles, and bareback. Wealthy Argentineans practice polo, scared children take their first pony walk, and riders of more experience hurtle over increasingly high obstacles on hunter-jumper courses. Horses in Los Angeles are used by police departments for crowd control and crime patrol, are ridden by celebrities for ceremonial parades, and, in addition to providing recreation for families, are sometimes used as proof of social status.

In 1995, the total number of horses in the county, according to the health department, was approximately 150,000, a number that's been declining ever since due to the rapidly inflating property values. It's just getting too expensive to devote land to barns, stables, and trails. You wouldn't know it on my street, however. In addition to "Savannah," the chestnut American thoroughbred that belongs to the landlady in back, my neighbors on the left have two horses, and on the right three. Almost all the people around me ride in Griffith Park, and the smell of hay and horseshit in the mornings is so strong you'd swear I lived on a ranch.

During the mid-1980s, the City of Burbank had a fit of "master planning." As might be expected of a process bearing such dominant nomenclature, it led to a proposal to eliminate this unique attribute of the community, the presence of horses within city limits. Urban planners proposed that such quaint reminders of Burbank's agricultural past should make way for other kinds of development, ones that would create higher property values and increase the tax base. The homeowners fought back and won the right to an R-1-H zoning designation—residential horse-keeping properties—for the area bound on the west by the movie studios, on the south by the park, and on the east and north by two major commercial boulevards. The Rancho Equestrian today contains more than two hundred homes and is one of a number of equestrian neighborhoods that, as the writer Don Waldie pointed out to me, tend to be located on the banks of either the Los Angeles or the San Gabriel river, both of which afford rights-of-way for public trails.

Horses are the iconic animals of Hollywood, the MGM lion and the puma in the park notwithstanding. And movies have everything to do with their status, another kind of narrative continuity—a historical one—that helps orient the local community at the social as well as at the individual level.

As I trundle back down across the ninety-acre landfill to rejoin the steeply graded access road, the susurrations of the small gas pumps every few yards pass in one ear and out the other. The waist-high units are feeding the gas from the rotting material under my feet to the nearby generators. Here, the average depth of the residential garbage, tree trimmings, and construction waste is around 290 feet: twenty-seven years' worth of carrot peelings, lawn clippings, and broken drywall. These little vertical extraction wells daily capture 3.5 million cubic feet of methane and other vapors for burning in the generating station. It's hard to understand how large the landfill is until you compare the topology on this side of the ridge with the sister canyon over the hill. When you envision the entirety of Royce's Canyon being filled to the brim with garbage, you get some idea of how much it took to fill Toyon Canyon.

Nowadays, our garbage is shipped out to new landfills farther out, but the tree trimmings go into city composting facilities, one of which is on a hillside below me. The Los Angeles urban forest, covering more than 485 square miles, contains an estimated ten million trees, of which two million are maintained by public agencies. The Street Tree Division, part of the City of L.A. Bureau of Street Services, removes ten thousand tons of green waste from some ninety thousand trees trimmed every year and recycles all of it as mulch that's then spread out on city landscaping, such as street medians. In a city as large as Los Angeles—a machine that produces almost 1 percent of the planet's greenhouse emissions—civic nature becomes an industrial process.

Only hikers, equestrians, and city workers traverse these terraces, the sere slope a scar that will remain visible on the hillside for miles around for years and years—although, ironically, it is invisible to most passersby. Even when the landfill is green in spring, the architectonic shaping and gradient of its face doesn't fit our innate conception of a parkland, that genetic template we developed over millions of years as primates on the African savanna to recognize a healthy landscape. As a result, most people unconsciously don't process it visually at all. It's just an empty, brown field on the hills. The slope is just more industrial nature that doesn't fit our preconceived notion of either park or wilderness held in reserve for recreation.

Park to landfill to cemetery to Disney, freeway overpasses and horse trail underpasses, mountain lion to Mickey Mouse, all in one short walk. The conjunctions are so compressed that they form their own continuum, again something that we comment on only occasionally, so ubiquitous are the seemingly absurd concatenations here. Part of the reason we accept and then ignore them so easily is that we have been conditioned by film and television to assimilate such disjunctive experiences, a compression in space equal to the one created in time. In movies, we leap within seconds from a scene in New York City to one in Tokyo (although both of which may have actually been filmed in locations in Los Angeles). On television, we watch a broadcast that switches from a war in Iraq to a speech given on the steps of the White House to an advertisement for an SUV careening over a polar icescape.

Likewise, to live in Los Angeles is to suffer from a pervasive sense of déjà vu, so many movies have been filmed here. Just in Griffith Park, for example, I pass by locations for James Dean's *Rebel Without a Cause;* an early version of *The Three Musketeers,* starring John Wayne; the first *Terminator;* two Batman movies (his lair is a cave in one of the park's hillsides); and the original *Invasion of the Body Snatchers.* My favorite use of the park in film was the mid-1930s serial *The Phantom Empire,* starring Gene Autry, a sci-fi Western wherein "America's favorite singing cowboy" defended his Radio Ranch from robots controlled by the queen of an underground city.

In honor of the cowboy actor, when I return to my car, I decide to take the long way home, driving down past the Los Angeles Zoo to come out almost at the front door of the Museum of the American West, an organization founded in 1988 by the performer and his wife. Autry left his imprimatur on the museum's mission statement to "exhibit and interpret the heritage of the West, and show how it has influenced America and the world." I think it would be more accurate to say that the place exhibits a mostly unspoken fascination with how we conflate nature and culture, time and place.

I pull in under the young sycamore trees in the parking lot and amble through the pastel neo-Spanish arches fronting the museum, a set piece designed to evoke California's southwestern heritage. The complex is really just an unassuming collection of boxes—galleries, offices, and support spaces—that have been dressed to the exacting standards of Hollywood as a themed monument to the history of the state. Along with various changing exhibitions on the ground floor, a permanent display of movie and television props used by Autry and his colleagues is housed on the floor below, a curious trove of the real and the fake. Genuine Colt revolvers from 1881 and a single-shot cavalry model Springfield carbine reside next to prop arrows with rubber arrowheads and the ubiquitous necessity of every saloon in the West, sheets of breakaway glass. I'm particularly partial to the Texas Ranger badge used by Clayton Moore when he played the Lone Ranger, and a pair of white, goat-hair chaps used in Buffalo Bill's Wild West Show.

Autry was born in Oklahoma in 1907 and was discovered by Will Rogers, the internationally renowned cowboy humorist and film star who was living on a ranch at the foot of the Santa Monica Mountains. Autry started performing on the radio in 1928, debuted in films in 1934, and, six years later, was the fourth-highest-grossing movie actor in the country. He retired from film in 1953 after starring in ninety-three movies, but was already three years into his eponymous television show. He remained active in TV until the late 1980s, even as he was planning for the museum that would house his personal collection of Western art and related Hollywood memorabilia.

I sat next to Autry at a dinner at the museum one night in 1997, about a year before he passed away. His wife, Jackie, was there, as were several old friends. Autry was resplendent in a Western suit and bola tie, a slightly roguish gentleman recounting stories about horse racing. He was as proud of the museum that bore his name as a Guggenheim or a Getty would have been. The permanent galleries downstairs—where Bierstadt and Remington paintings hang next to the silver-inlaid saddles and antique firearms—were at the time arranged in a linear narrative illustrating how America implemented what it took to be its Manifest Destiny during the nineteenth and early twentieth centuries. It was a story dominated by the traditional characters, white Euro-American males, and thus skewed toward presentation versus interpretation, which nurtured a sort of historical pareidolia. Even then, though, the curatorial staff of the museum had long-range ambitions to widen the scope of the collection and programming.

When the museum first opened, it received mixed reviews. Aficionados of Autry films and Western horse culture loved it; art and culture critics dismissed it somewhat gently as a vanity project. Very quietly, however, the staff would begin assembling exhibitions that favored a revisionist history of the West, ones that explored the roles played by women, Jews, and Chinese, among others. In 2002, the museum absorbed the Web-based Women of the West Museum and then, a year later, announced another merger, this time with the oldest museum in Los Angeles, the Southwest American Museum of the Indian. The Southwest Museum houses one of the most significant collections of Native American artifacts in the country. The newly rechristened Autry National Center has recently established a research institute to more fully involve scholars with the combined collections, libraries, and archives, and the curators are rearranging the center's permanent collections to reflect a less linear view of history—one that accommodates the multiple conjunctions, layers, and competing myths of the West.

What the singing cowboy will have left behind, then, won't simply be handsome artifacts buttressing simplified versions of cowboys versus Indians and the closing of the American frontier, but a much more complicated, ongoing investigation into the interpenetration of culture and nature. Since much of our view of the West has been shaped by film and television for a century, it seems almost inevitable that such an effort would be undertaken by a museum with one foot in the industry.

Autry played a large part in the shaping of the twentieth-century myth of the cowboy. That is, his role as a cowboy actor externalized our hopes and fears about the relationships between the city and the wilderness. *The Phantom Empire*, the Autry serial film that preceded *Flash Gordon* and other science-fiction classics, is a prime example. That some of its scenes were filmed in Bronson Canyon, at the southwest corner of Griffith Park, as well as at Griffith Observatory, is a good trope for the relationship of the park itself with L.A. To summarize: Autry runs Radio Ranch, the headquarters for his daily radio show and a rural retreat for urban kids who need sunshine, fresh air, and a healthy dose of horseback riding. Unbeknownst to him, two thousand feet below the surface sits the ancient "Scientific City" of Murania, which is rich in radium. A group of evil researchers convince Autry to help them find the city so that they can strip-mine its ore, which leads the Murania queen to order her robots into action against the cowboy broadcaster. Although the queen plots to murder Autry numerous times, when the robots attempt to rebel against her, Autry saves the queen and destroys the robots.

The cowboy myth being promulgated in the series is a surprisingly poignant variation. Cowboys have become a breed of men who have exhausted their original role as herders of cattle and transferred the use of their skills in the outdoors into media production and social work, seeking to counter the ill effects of urbanization. At the same time, this focus puts these Western heroes into conflict with technological progress, and they would rather support a good old-fashioned human tyrant than moral robots. The cowboy has moved from trying to subdue wilderness—in the parlance of the nineteenth century, "the home of the naked savage"—to running a theme park about nature for kids, but he is then forced to defend the park from technology, as exemplified by a new breed of savages (albeit metal ones), the robots.

When I leave the museum, I follow the drive as it curves around the zoo and the northern end of the park. I wonder if the mountain lion, presumably sleeping somewhere above me during the daytime, keeps an eye on the facilities. We've come a long way since Autry played a former forest ranger in the 1949 *Riders of the Whistling Pines,* a movie in which he took potshots at a puma. Rangers today are more interested in tracking the movements of the cats in the Santa Monicas with GPS radio collars than eliminating the animals, which makes Griffith Park a very different kind of Radio Ranch. The biggest danger facing the cougars is that they cannot move easily enough among the local mountain ranges to maintain a population sufficient for breeding. By using high-frequency communications bounced off satellites to determine how the cats travel, the rangers can determine where to set aside wildlife corridors. Tunnels allowing the mountain lions and other species, such as bobcats and gray foxes, which face the same problems, to bypass the freeway systems are slowly gaining approval in the region.

This is a radical revision of the relationship we have with remnants of what was once a major predator in the local mountains. It's a deliberate effort to preserve and increase coexisting populations of different species in a world that is increasingly landscaped, that is, fragmented, by humans. And urban horses, I am convinced, should be seen as part of that effort. Larger and less domestic than dogs and cats, these large animals connect us both to history and to a story that is not ours, that is prehuman, or that is, in a more romanticized term, prelapsarian.

Throughout *The Phantom Empire* series, Autry's career, and the history of movies, the horse has been presented as an animal that acts in partnership with people, whether as the mount of an Indian, a cowboy, a soldier, or a frontiersman or as the work animal of a settler, a farmer, or the owner of a dry-goods store in town. It takes no large powers of observation to note that the reins of the horses, at least in terms of who is riding in the hills above L.A. today and who first spotted the mountain lions, have passed to women. But regardless of the identity of the horseback rider, male or female, rancher or clerk, the partnership lifts the person into a new relationship with the world, providing a higher vantage point from which to view the world and to share in a wider understanding of it, if not sometimes to gain power over it. This changed view may have something to do with how riding a horse extends one's sense of peripersonal space.

Personal space is the volume your body occupies; *extrapersonal* space is the area that lies beyond your reach. *Peripersonal* space is what is in between, where you can reach with your hands or tools, the brain actually adjusting its conception of this space to account for artificial extensions of reach. Pick up a screwdriver, and your brain will recast its mental map of the world to include your suddenly increased ability to reach a foot farther than you could before. Put on a tall hat, and your body will know how far you have to bend your knees to get through a low doorway. Put on bulky clothes, and you will feel your sense of mass adjust.

The ability of your mind to respond to a longer reach or a larger body extends to horses—and to cars. When you're riding, the feet of your mount become extensions of your own, and you feel the terrain ahead of you along with the horse. You feel as if you share the horse's body. As for automobiles—think of how you feel when someone dents your car. It more than angers you; it almost hurts physically. The skin of the car has become yours. Road rage on the freeways during rush hour isn't simply a by-product of frustration, but also one of perceived personal space. The car's sheet metal becomes your skin, and other drivers threaten to touch you, to invade your personal space without invitation. You instinctively want to push back.

The most vivid instance of road rage that I've seen lately, however, was earlier today between a horseback rider crossing Hollywood Drive and a man in a Lexus. The woman was descending from the trail leading down from the landfill, the coupe cresting the gap near where I had my car parked. Horseback riders know to listen as well as watch for speeding cars, but the young guy in the sports car was visibly startled by the horse. He slowed just in time to receive a plentiful helping of verbal abuse from the person towering a good six feet above him. He crept down the other side of the hill thoroughly chastened, a reminder of how police can use horses to such good effect in crowd control.

The intersection of cars and horses is ongoing. The Spanish first came into the San Fernando Valley in the mid-1700s and, by the 1790s, had established the local mission and begun carving up the terrain into *ranchos,* or territory. Until the late 1890s, when the first car came into the valley over Cahuenga Pass from Los Angeles, horses were the primary mode of personal transportation. When World War II ended, suburbanization began to rapidly transform farm fields, orchards, and pastures into subdivisions, and the conversion from horseback to automobile seemed virtually complete—or so it would seem when you're cruising down Van Nuys Boulevard.

In reality, however, the horses never went away completely, and in places such as Griffith Park, they have reclaimed the landscape. Likewise on the dirt roads in the Verdugo Mountains across the way from me. Rusted street signs still sit atop the highest ridge, but the only vehicles allowed into the mountains anymore are those driven by firefighters, and the asphalt on the lower slopes abrades away. By shifting my place in Los Angeles, whether it is from an apartment complex to an oil field, from a cemetery to an observatory, from a subdivision to a park, I am also shifting my place in time. If we use time to express the vastness of outer space, we sometimes take space to express time.

We measure the direction of and progress along time's arrow by visible changes that "take place" around us. Change place, and you will experience different kinds and rates of change. In Burbank, when I'm walking around the neighborhood at dusk and one of the local horses tugs at its reins to come over and greet me with a friendly nuzzle, my experience of the city and how I perceive the place's relationship to nature are shifted. It's no longer simply the early twenty-first century, but a more complex and layered temporal situation.

If our perception of peripersonal space is changed by what we hold in our hands, what we wear, what we ride—I wonder if we also have a peripersonal sense of time. I wonder how, if we begin to more fully inhabit the space around us, we might also enlarge our sense of time and extend our reach within it. Scientists who study how we experience time and space know that, if our sense of time is compromised by neurological damage or drugs, we will also undergo a change in how we experience space, which then seems to either lose or gain dimensions.

Under either pathological or profound meditative states, people who feel as if they are experiencing the past, present, and future simultaneously also feel space to be infinite.

In 1846, Walt Whitman, upon viewing daguerreotype portraits, wrote that time and space were annihilated for the viewer by this technological identification of semblance with reality. Contemporary culture, which is largely defined through multiple photographic media, seeks to collapse our experience of time and space within a constant collision of episodic appearances mediated through every kind of broadcast. The indiscriminately communal experience of billboards, television, film, and the Internet maximizes our ability to sell things to one another, whether it is new fashions in apparel, tourism, or music. We create desire by making all time and space look as though they are available all the time, everywhere. You can be anyone at any time experiencing anything you want, if you are willing to pay for it. Sadly, as with any addiction, the more we avail ourselves of such transformations, the less excitement we experience. All too soon, all our experiences threaten to become one and the same. Our appetite for difference in time and space becomes insatiable. It's not enough to be tourists in space, but we strive to own time, and we appropriate the images of earlier eras at will, from the cowboy West to ancient Egypt. What the spiral of desire-satiation-desire leads us to create is the endless present. We are flatlining time.

The French writer Guy Debord published his seminal book on the collapse of space and time in contemporary culture, *Society of the Spectacle,* in 1967. "This society which eliminates geographical distance reproduces distance internally as spectacular separation," he cautioned, a succinct formulation of exactly what most movies do. He was also talking about temporal distance, otherwise defined as history. He warned that a society addicted to such practices—to spectacle for its own sake—ignores genuine history. The society thus becomes "frozen" in time and increasingly isolated from nature. Its citizens live in an artificial "perpetual present."

When we think about verb tenses in English—when we think about them at all, which is seldom—we remember three: a past, a present, and a future. We seldom consider the fifteen to twenty-five others (depending on how you break them out). We remember the simple past: "I saw a movie." Or the simple future: "I will see a movie tomorrow." Or the present tense: "I am watching the movie." But among the many variations we have of linking time into compound tenses, there is the present perfect continuous: "I have been watching this movie for an hour." This tense, also known as the present perfect progressive, expresses something that began in the past and has continued up to the present. It can also contain the future: "I have been watching this movie for an hour, and I have no idea when it will end."

We like living in the present and admire it so much that we write books about living for the moment, the importance of living in the here and now. It's a mind-set perfectly appropriate for a cinematic culture. Movies bring their time and space to us, and we live in them for the time being. In cinema, whatever its time and space, be they ancient Rome or Mars in the far future, we are there. And that time is always happening right now, in the present, as we live and breath. We seldom remember we're in a movie theater on a Sunday afternoon unless someone's cell phone rings, and then we are extremely resentful of being pulled out of that stretched sense of the present.

In classical physics, Sir Isaac Newton described motion as

a change in position over time. Sitting in a movie theater abrogates our experience of that calculation to some degree. The world moves in front of us, but we do not. I like to walk because it is a slow enough way of being in motion that we remain conscious of being in motion. We experience change not just in what we see, but on our skins, with changing temperatures and atmospheric pressures, in our noses and in our ears; it is not someone else's time, but ours. We are active in the creation of time, versus passive receivers of it.

It's no accident that people say Los Angeles has no nature and no past, the two being considered coterminous conditions by many Americans. Walking in Los Angeles, the most powerful nexus of cinematic process in human history, affords me an opportunity to see for myself how the city is inseparable from and animated by both nature and history. I am thus reminded that we can and must individually reconstruct time and space no matter where we are. We have to rescue our sense of them from trivialization—from perceiving them as mere commodities to be bought and experienced at our leisure—or we will lose our sense of difference. This is a project considerably complicated by Hollywood, which increasingly manipulates time and space to satisfy our desire for narrative, for a story that has a beginning and a middle and an end and that we can experience in the present. A straight narrative is very unlike life, which for each of us begins and ends in the middle of everyone else's stories.

As they say in the movies . . . to be continued.

MODEL BEHAVIOR

A sandbox, according to the somewhat deficient definition in *The New Oxford American Dictionary,* is "a shallow box or hollow in the ground partly filled with sand for children to play in." I say deficient because I have been spending my time lately around a couple of very large sandboxes filled with adults and nary a child in sight. I'm not talking about public playgrounds, nor those playpens used by grown-ups to get in touch with their inner child, although we need to visit that latter topic before proceeding. Our collective behavior in these enclosed analogues for nature might reveal something about how we as a society relate to time.

In 1911, the novelist H. G. Wells wrote a book called *Floor Games* in which he described how, while building miniature islands and cities with his sons, he came to better know the boys. This was because they acted out their feelings about relationships in the family—feelings that they would otherwise have left unspoken or that had even been otherwise unknown to themselves. He followed it up two years later with *Little Wars,* which instructed readers how to conduct tabletop maneuvers at a scale of 1 to 32. I hesitate to speculate on what that says about his family life, but note that the author, a renowned pacifist, published the book just in time to prepare a generation of boys for the horrors of World War I, which commenced the next summer.

Twenty years later, Margaret Lowenfeld, an early British adherent of Freud, was inspired by the two books to use "sand trays" with model houses and vehicles as she attempted to navigate the psyches of children. She called this the "world technique," as her charges built up elaborate realms in which they expressed both conscious and unconscious thoughts. Dora Kalff, who had studied with Lowenfeld, was encouraged by Carl Jung in the 1950s to develop a therapy based on "sandplay." Jung considered play one of the most profound ways to tap into subconscious archetypes, an idea supported by electrocardiogram (EKG) studies in the 1960s. The tests showed more electrical activity taking place in the brain during play than during any other human activity, including sex. Manipulating objects and symbols in a small sand tray roughly thirty by twenty inches is recognized internationally now as a therapeutic technique valid for both children and adults.

The sandboxes I have been observing are larger and variously devoted to exploding, burning up, and otherwise destroying scale models and to the exploration of that red planet named after the god of war, Mars. None of the people involved have anything therapeutic in mind, but it is clear that they are having an immense amount of fun with very expensive toys. Their game is the fine art of manipulating our perceptions of time and space through special effects for entertainment and science.

On a warm August evening, I drive to Van Nuys so I can witness my friend Bob Hurrie blow up a French village in the first of the two sandboxes. All summer long, I've been watching his crew painstakingly "re-create" what is in "reality" a "fictional" town, and now that the model is finished, it's time to destroy the village in six seconds or less. I put the three words in quotes to remind myself to remind the reader of how relative the terms are, as they are defined here almost exclusively in relationship to one another.

Hurrie, a man of medium build in his early sixties with a thick mane of gray hair to his shoulders, was trained in visual special effects (VFX) by Douglas Trumbull, the genius behind the appearance of numerous science-fiction classics, among them *2001: A Space Odyssey, Close Encounters of the Third Kind,* and *Blade Runner.* While working for Trumbull in New York, Hurrie was lured away by Doug Smith, another special-effects director, who was designing the Egyptian theme for the Luxor Hotel-Casino in Las Vegas. Afterward, Smith brought him to L.A. to work on the largest model-movie ever made, the 1996 invasion blockbuster *Independence Day.* Hurrie had started out as an independent filmmaker in New York and never wanted to work in L.A., but, he admitted, "If you work in the movies, you can't avoid it." *ID4,* as the movie is known in the business because of its July 4 release date, won an Oscar for its special effects, and Hurrie has been here ever since. These days, he works for Mike Joyce, who owns Cinema Production Services (CPS), a business fifteen minutes west of Burbank on the freeway.

CPS occupies a 22,000-square-foot warehouse that you enter through a modest reception area. I walk by the offices and pass posters for *Mars Attacks, True Lies, Terminator 2,* and *Batman Returns,* just some of the company's previous VFX jobs. Behind the offices, the ceiling rises to 26 feet high. On either side of the cavernous and dim workshop space that I've entered are stacked scale models of everything from spaceships and submarines to a hemisphere of the moon and Victorian buildings from *Peter*

Pan. The right half of the floor is occupied by a dozen work-benches and a paint station. The left half holds a 30-foot-long zeppelin, its fragile bronze foil girders covered with more than three hundred pieces of silk-span paper glued by hand over the armature. A tiny gunner's nest is perched atop what in real life was an aircraft 640 feet long. It would have been like flying on a cloud to occupy that seat, at least until the British fighters showed up.

Hurrie has spent the last three months supervising the construction of a model set and miniature aircraft for *Flyboys*, a production directed by Tony Bill and starring the French actor Jean Reno. The movie is about the Lafayette Escadrille—the American pilots who volunteered for the French military in World War I before the United States officially joined the fight. The film's budget will make it "the most expensive inexpensive movie" ever filmed, according to Bill, who is quoted as saying that he is trying to make a $150 million movie for $60 million.

The Germans built only eighty-eight of the lighter-than-air dirigibles, which were held aloft by cells of, unfortunately, flammable hydrogen. Massively streamlined, the airships were nearly as fast as the airplanes being built at the beginning of the war. Once fighter planes were developed as a specialized genre, however, it spelled the end of the zeppelin's usefulness for reconnaissance and bombing. The movie will feature live-action dogfights flown over England, but detonating full-scale zeppelins and villages isn't within the budget: hence the role of CPS.

The talented staff of CPS took months to build the model zeppelin, but the model will be blown up in a matter of only a few seconds with a gas bomb loaded with black powder, a combination that will look like a hydrogen explosion. Hurrie and the crew will shoot the action from four angles with separate cameras running 120 frames per second—the normal rate is 24 frames per second (fps) for real-time projection—so all told, the action will constitute about 50 seconds of film, which is a lot for a movie. After all, an entire day holds only 86,400 seconds. You can assemble motion in your mind from rates as low as 10 fps, but the flicker of alternating light and dark during projection will drive you nuts. The flicker disappears around 16 fps. If you both shoot and then project film at 24 fps, you get what the mind interprets as smooth and uninterrupted action occurring at normal speed. The faster you run the film through the camera, while keeping the projection at that same speed, the slower the motion becomes. When you blow up things, the action in real life is so fast that the audience would miss it if it weren't slowed down.

A few days earlier, I had stopped to watch Paul Steeves gluing up one-quarter- and one-eighth-scale machine guns. He was surrounded by a half dozen model Fokker DR-1 triplanes—the plane the Red Baron flew as an ace in World War I. Steeves earned a degree in industrial design, worked in special effects for a while, but then spent five years in the U.S. Marine Corps. His military stint included nine months in Iraq as a helicopter crew chief. When he returned home and applied to get back into the business, he accepted an offer from Mike Joyce because he wanted to work on this particular movie. "Back into flight, so to speak," he says with a grin. Steeves is stocky, clean-cut, affable, and wearing a gray T-shirt. He still looks a little like a marine.

"The thing about an explosion is that it happens instantly," he says. "The movies slow it all down so you can actually see it; you can see the flames going from one end of the zeppelin to another. In real life, it's not like that. It happens and it's over. Then you figure out what happened." I imagine he knows what he's talking about.

So, you film explosions in slow motion from several different viewpoints at the same time, then edit them all together to get, well, the most bang for your buck. And I'm here this evening to watch a fair portion of the *Flyboys* budget go up in smoke, which will happen behind the huge black drape that separates the shooting stage from the workshop. Behind the floor-to-ceiling barrier is a sixty-foot-square platform painted matte chocolate and covered with decomposed granite from a nursery supply business. The sandbox. They've spread out the coarse, golden sand by hand and smoothed it with a broom, then sprinkled over it some darker dirt. This "ground" surrounds the dozen buildings of a French town that has been captured by the Germans and turned into an ammo dump, all of it built at one-eighth scale, or 1½ inches to the foot.

Telephone poles strung with tiny wires cross the set, and antiaircraft guns and artillery emplacements are surrounded with model barbed wire. In the story, the town has already been bombed once. In addition to the very artful, natural warping of the individual roof shingles—thousands of them glued down by hand just so—some of the roofs were built with holes in them. Hundreds of tiny sandbags are stacked here and there. An ancient train engine waits on a siding, ready to receive the bombs stockpiled around the premises. I climb up on a catwalk to look down on the village, a view equivalent to being about a hundred feet in the air, and catch myself looking for people. Very small people who would look just the right size walking in and out of the knee-high buildings.

On the east side of the stage is a motor-controlled filming

system with an eighteen-foot arm. The entire assembly can move in four directions and rotate, and the head that holds the camera can tilt. The machinery is anchored very securely to the concrete floor so shots that are repeated will register precisely. On the south side is an even larger rig resting on portable rails. CPS owns a half dozen cameras, most of them devoted to running film at the high speeds necessary for pyrotechnic work. They can shoot up to 120 fps or more when the crew is blowing things up, which is what this stage was built to do.

"You might do a shot for the action, then another for fill light, then a smoke scene, and it all has to match," Hurrie tells me. "When we were working on *ID4* in the Howard Hughes hangar at Playa del Rey, the microscopic movement of the beach sand under the building threw it off. It's that sensitive when you're layering this stuff in a digital master during postproduction." I realize, as Hurrie is speaking, one reason why movies are so expensive to make. It's insanely difficult to match time and motion when you are constructing events artificially, then filming them at enough angles so the human mind will be presented with a picture so comprehensive that the scene is believable and won't be rejected out of hand.

Then there are the lights. I count sixty-three of them aimed directly at the set or indirectly through reflectors. Out front, a generator chugs away, its current brought back here through five thick cables to supplement the juice brought in through the wall panel. "There's six hundred amps in the wall and fourteen hundred from the generator, both of which are maxed out," explains Hurrie. "We have to use an incredible amount of light to compensate for speed—if you're shooting film at eight times twenty-four frames per second, you need eight times the amount of light. It gets so hot in here you can fry an egg on the set. See those two largest lights?" Hurrie points to large cans mounted on tall poles at the far side. "They're twenty thousand watts each. We leave them off as much as possible. It's not just because it's already hot in here, but we don't want to cook the pyro."

Ah, yes, the pyro. John Sturber, the leader of the pyro team, wears a T-shirt from his alma mater, the U.S. Navy Seals. He's on his hands and knees overseeing the wiring of the forty-three trip switches on a piece of track laid out parallel to the south side of the set for the larger rig. For this shot—one that will show the effects of two airplanes bombing the town into oblivion—two guys will hand-push the larger rig with its thirty-eight-foot boom along those rails, covering more than fifty feet in about six seconds. On the set, an older gentleman putters about, placing sixty separate charges in the buildings and small holes in the "ground." He takes a small plastic bag out of a box, shakes it gently to mix the contents, places it into a fist-sized mortar, and inserts the wires for detonation. Another guy is wiring up primer cord on the undersides of the roofs so that they will blow up properly along with the primary charges. It would be unfortunate, indeed, were the lights to be too hot.

In addition to the camera overhead on the boom, two cameras are on the floor and are mounted to short tripods and braced with clamps, which will give the audience an eye-level view of the action. When the shot is made, that's where I'll be standing, just behind and to one side of the ground cameras and near one of the numerous fire extinguishers placed strategically around the set. The extinguisher is an unusual piece of playground equipment not found next to most sandboxes, to be sure.

Around nine o'clock, the crew starts rolling the boom and camera forward a few inches at a time, watching its progress over the set through monitors. As the rig moves down the track, it will trip switches mounted alongside the rails that will, in turn, set off the charges in sequence. Sturber refers constantly to a digital photo that was taken from the catwalk and that looks remarkably like an aerial photo of a real town. Little squares of blue tape stuck to the photo are numbered for each charge. By watching how the aerial view advances in the monitor, he decides in what order to mount the switches so that the sequence of the explosions will look as if bombs are falling singly and in pairs from two aircraft flying over the village.

Peter Chiang, the VFX supervisor for *Flyboys,* watches with Sturber, and they work it out together. Chiang has not worked on a shot like this before and is concerned that there might be too many charges within such a small space and time. Sturber reminds him that up to 10 percent of the pyrotechnics will fail to go off. The camera progresses overhead, the pieces of tape get moved around, and crew members mark the tracks every few feet to guide the mounting of the switches.

Denny McHugh, the director of photography, has decided to run the overhead camera at 60 fps, and the two locked-off cameras on the floor at 72 fps. The passage over the town will take almost three times as long on camera as the actual shoot. That aerial view will slow down the appearance of bombs blowing up on the ground below, but the action as viewed at ground level—the viewpoint the audience will identify with the most—will be slowed down even more. By editing together all three views, the director will create a cinematic experience many times longer than the actual event. It will be believable, yet even as stretched out as it will be, when the audience watches it, the scene will seem to be over in a flash, such being the relativity of time and motion in a movie.

It's not until just after midnight that the last of the charges are set, the roofs are glued back down on the miniature build-ings, and everyone's footprints erased from the dirt. The crew has been here since eight this morning, and the pyro guys are obviously beat, which adds a certain element of anxiety to the proceedings. Crossed wires and all that.

At 12:30, Chiang checks the height of the camera overhead with a handheld laser and has it adjusted four inches higher. Then Hurrie, who has been watching quietly all evening, takes over. Most of the time, his job is to be a professional worrier, to coordinate everything while managing to stay out of the way, a job he conducts with aplomb. Now he assumes his role as assistant director, and there's an authority in his voice I've not heard before. He's already cleared out most of the crew, leav-ing on the set only himself, the director of photography, two people manning fire extinguishers, the two lads who will push the dolly, and me.

The first thing Hurrie does is brief everyone on how to get out of the building in case of a fire. My escape route would involve my navigating clear around the set to the far corner. I note that Hurrie has positioned next to me a crew member who has used a fire extinguisher before. Thank you, Bob. Sturber reminds us that fire is slow, that there's nothing highly com-bustible here—so we should take our time if we have to get out. Rushing either to fight a fire or to evacuate is when people get hurt. Thank you, John.

At 12:47, Hurrie tells all of us to put in our earplugs. He calls out commands, confirming that everyone is set, and orders the video to roll (actually a digital camera with a computer moni-tor located just off the set). He calls for the film cameras to roll and then, last of all, to make the pyro hot. His arm drops. The camera rig is off and running down the track.

The guys push the camera for four feet before they hit a

switch, so it seems that time is passing and nothing is happening. Then the first two charges go off at the other side of the sandbox. Twin fireballs blossom in the air over the buildings, and the explosions begin to march toward me, getting larger and larger. One, two, left, right. A building is blown apart, a truck, another building. A vehicle flies through the air. Smoke is everywhere. A charge goes off right in front of me with a loud bang, throwing dirt in the air, and I'm waiting for the next one—and it's over.

The air is acrid and black ash floats down. Everyone is silent while looking for signs of fire. There are none. The big exhaust fan is turned on to clear the carcinogens, and we all go out to see the digital version on the monitor. Which is nothing short of amazing. Watching the overhead shot, you feel as if you are in a plane flying over the town as it explodes beneath you. The pattern of the falling bombs mimics perfectly the flight path of your vantage point. And from the two ground cameras, it's the real deal, at least as we have been taught to see it on film. That last explosion tosses dirt right at the lens. Very real. Everyone claps and congratulates Sturber on a successful shoot, and the pyro guys step up on the stage to disarm any unexploded charges.

I clap Hurrie on the shoulder. He has his hands full with shutting down the set for the night, so I leave, walking by a small, alien spaceship built for the movie *Zathura*. The director of the film liked the spacecraft so much that he had asked Mike Joyce if he could have it for his living room, and it's out on the loading dock to be picked up. It's startling but not uncommon to walk into a house in the Hollywood Hills and confront a prop you've seen in a film, which lends some veracity to the nickname Hollyweird.

The explosions tonight were a thrill to experience, but this transformation of action on a miniaturized set and through a lens into what looks like genuine wartime footage is hair-raising. No cute weirdness there. When they add sound, the disbelief of audiences will be nowhere to be found. In moviemaking, there's an enormous tension in creating something that's real but that represents something else that's not real. Remember those words I put in quotes? The *reality* here is the sequence of little explosions done now, but the realism depicts large explosions from ninety years ago—a past that never happened. The trick is to make the audience suspend its normative disbelief so that people will have a collective emotional reaction to what they're seeing, be it lava flowing down Wilshire Boulevard or a part of France being cratered. Succeed, and the movie may make hundreds of millions of dollars. Fail, and you lose everything but your tax deductions.

Filmgoing—sitting in a movie theater—is like attending the performance of a symphony. Both are aesthetic experiences over which the audience has no control, a rarity in the digital age, and you'd better get your money's worth. If the manipulation of time and space works, you are embraced by the film's sequence, the continuity that it provides, and you go along for the ride. All of us are surrounded by the everyday chaos of life and construct narratives to make sense of it all. We're suckers for being handed ready-made stories, and we quite willingly suspend our disbelief, given any good excuse to do so. Ironically, however, we need just a touch of chaos even in a movie for it to appear real. One day, I sat next to Mike Joyce while he was working on the one-quarter-scale model airplanes for which Paul was prepping the machine guns. Joyce held up a biplane, frowned at a wing, and dabbed paint on it.

"Quarter-scale is a real sweet scale to blow up things in," he explained. "It holds details. Scale's dictated ultimately, if money's not a problem, by what action needs to be accomplished. If you have unlimited money and you're doing mostly pyro, bigger is better. You get to a certain size, however, and you might as well blow up the real thing."

I asked Joyce how many shops around L.A. still did model pyro work, thinking about the increasing use of digital special effects. "Half the shops like us have gone out of business in the last five years, from maybe a dozen down to four or five. The studios helped build up the film industry in places like New Zealand and Australia, and now a lot of the work is done offshore. But we'll be in business doing earthquakes and explosions for years. CG—computer graphics—can do great stuff, but you lose the random events, the quality of the unforeseen, and the effects of nature and gravity. Like when we dropped a model truck off a forty-foot cliff and a door accidentally opened and got blown up past the camera lens. Boy, that looked just fantastic, but you could never plan that. Pyro in CG just looks manipulated."

I keep that word *manipulation* in mind as a few days later I head in the opposite direction from home, east to behind the Verdugo Mountains and over to the foothills of the San Gabriels in La Cañada Flintridge, a community that sits next to Pasadena and close to the bottom of Mount Wilson. In 1936, some local rocket enthusiasts and students from the California Institute of Technology went into the Arroyo Seco, a dry wash not far from my destination, and tried to launch a model rocket on Halloween. They survived the ensuing fire. By their fourth attempt, they at least achieved ignition—although they melted the apparatus.

They soon moved their efforts onto campus, but after several unplanned explosions, the Suicide Squad was asked to return to the arroyo. Thus was the seed planted for what would eventually become the Jet Propulsion Laboratory in 1944.

My father worked here in deep space communications during the early 1960s, just after JPL had been transferred from the U.S. Army to the still-fledgling National Aeronautics and Space Administration. My parents were divorced by then, but he would send me pictures of the huge dishes around the world through which signals are captured from spacecraft throughout the solar system. One evening, he drove me from Hollywood and over the hills to look down on the complex, which even then was impressive.

No rockets are launched anymore from JPL, which is managed by Cal Tech on behalf of NASA. The task of the lab's engineers is to build and operate unmanned spacecraft that the scientists use to bring back data from remote locations. Very remote locations, like Pluto. Tucked away in a large building on the 177-acre campus and visited by only a handful of the five-thousand-plus employees is a fifteen-square-foot enclosure—my second sandbox. It's one of the places where NASA goes to practice Mars. Two of the craft currently being run by JPL are the twin rovers wandering around the opposite sides of Mars, *Spirit* and *Opportunity*. A third sibling sits in the gritty test bed and is used to model driving options on the other planet. Before visiting the Mars sandbox, however, I'll start by looking at some of the images being processed from the far planet.

Guy Webster, a former science journalist from Phoenix who now works for media relations at the lab, meets me at the front desk and we walk over to the multistoried Space Flight Operations Facility. JPL looks like a college campus built in the 1960s,

mostly bland, modernist office buildings surrounded by eucalyptus trees and the oak woodlands of the arroyo. We enter
an unremarkable-looking building and take the elevator up to
the seventh floor and the Multimission Image Processing Lab
(MIPL), which in essence is where JPL does special effects.
Inside a quiet and low-ceilinged room filled with computer
monitors are seated the two people who conduct the complicated business of picturing Mars. We don't usually think of
science constructing false images in the quest for truth, but the
process of visually constructing Mars is just as manipulative
as what Mike Joyce and Bob Hurrie are doing, albeit from the
opposite direction. Hold that thought.

Doug Alexander, who has a background in geography from
the University of California at Santa Barbara, is the team lead
for image processing from the rovers, and Bob Deen is the chief
software engineer. Alexander has a young face and wears flip-
flops, but has gray in his barely visible goatee. Deen is a tall
and stout guy who can't keep his knees from bouncing with
an excess of nervous energy. While Alexander fills me in on the
flowchart for the imaging process, Deen can't wait to have me
look at the screen.

The rovers were launched from Earth in July 2003 and landed
in January 2004. They were tasked to last for ninety days and to
drive up to only three-quarters of a mile. That was reasonable,
given the rigors of Martian exploration, which include temperatures that plunge to 125°F below zero, corrosive chemicals in
the dust storms that plague the planet, and the vicissitudes of
running complicated engineering via remote control. By the
beginning of 2006 and to everyone's surprise, the rovers had
been driving around Mars for two Earth-years, had each traveled more than three miles, and together had sent back almost
130,000 images.

During the primary mission of the first ninety days, people here went to bed forty minutes later each day to account for the slightly longer Martian *sol* (the term scientists coined for the Martian day). They were required to keep the blinds down in the offices so they wouldn't see daylight or darkness, as the conflicting time cycles would interfere with their body chemistry and burn them out. "Walking with Mars," says Alexander. Some of the team members even wore both a custom watch designed to tell Martian time on one arm and a watch showing Earth time on the other. Nothing they did helped, and everyone was exhausted at the end of the three months. Now, the emphasis is on human sustainability, and the mission requirements are tailored more toward bankers' hours, but are still driven by mission demands.

Those demands remain strenuous. The people at MIPL gather information from various spacecraft, then format and standardize it into images that the science and engineering teams can analyze and compare. "We explode the bits and reconstruct them into image products," says Alexander. "The mission planning team and rover drivers extract navigation and terrain information—they can see where the vehicle is. We have to process the information during the Martian night so that the commands can be sent up the next morning." The two guys agree that they still tend to lose track of where in the week they are, an apt metaphor for how time is treated here.

Now, this is the thing about visual images—we assume they represent some aspect of simultaneity. For instance, when you take a picture with your digital camera, you believe you're capturing all the data right in front of it from a single moment. All the pixels are present and accounted for, and what you get is what you see. It looks as if you've captured a moment in time. This has little to do with how we actually see the world, however, which is a much slower and more cumulative process. Unlike snapping a picture, the Mars images processed by Alexander and Deen come together more like the way we see, and their work is a rough analogue for how the human mind constructs vision.

First, at this time of year and given the respective orbits of Earth and Mars, the delay in the time it takes a piece of data to get from Mars to here is about twenty minutes. That's how long it takes light and radio waves to travel the millions of miles between the two planets. The rovers each carry nine separate cameras that have different purposes, and images from the navigational cameras have priority, since the rovers can't move until JPL and NASA can analyze the pictures and plot their next move. So a rover takes a picture and then stores it until the orbiter circling the planet is within sight, since the rover itself doesn't have the power to send messages between the planets. The rover then broadcasts the images up to the orbiter for relay to Earth. The orbiter itself has to store the image until it can make a line-of-sight transmission to Earth, whereupon the data is received by one of three antennae in the Deep Space Network (one each in Australia, the Mojave Desert outside L.A., and Spain). From there the data is sent to JPL, sorted overnight by the guys, then given to the mission team, which decides how to react to where the rovers are. The team issues commands, which then have to travel back to Mars to be implemented.

The rovers creep around at a rate of less than one inch per second, and the most one of them has ever moved in a single day is 582 feet. When they execute a turn, it can take up to three days. So there's this aspect of "hurry up and wait" to the processing of the images. And that's the fast track for the navigational images. For the panoramic images that we're looking at, the rovers have to take many pictures over a period of days from one spot before starting the transmission process, and the data, which is of a lower priority than navigational digits, can sometimes wait in storage for weeks until there's time to process it.

These delays are analogous to how we each process the world. Think that what you see in front of you is in synch with when it's happening? Not so. There is a series of small delays that, when added together, create a gap of approximately 500 milliseconds (ms), or a half second, between an event and your perception of it. Light takes time to travel from, say, the face of the pretty girl or handsome guy you've just spied across the room to your eyes. Then there's the time it takes the light to be transformed in your eyes into electrical energy and be transmitted along the optic nerve into the cortex and processed. If you catch a glimpse of a person, or brush up against an object for less than 200 ms, you won't even be aware that you saw someone or touched anything. It takes a stimulus of at least 200 ms, plus 300 ms or so of processing, for the cortex to model an event so that it becomes part of your consciousness.

How we process reality is not at all simultaneous, although the mind is always taking in stimuli more quickly than it can process. The ability to see and react to facial features is among our quicker processing abilities that we've evolved, given its importance in sorting out friends and enemies, a primary survival tool. Experiments have shown that male subjects, when shown a picture of a female face so briefly that they can't even describe her features — so quickly (say, for 20 ms) that the subjects aren't even sure they were shown anything — the subjects could still ascertain accurately whether the woman was pretty. *Mindsight*, it's called, proof that the world is happening in advance of our perception of it.

Picking apart this processing of images from Mars with Deen

and Alexander is a bit like dissecting how our brains handle everyday sight, which has everything to do with interval and duration—with time. Likewise, how the engineers and scientists filter what they receive is somewhat like our mental manipulation of what we see. Each image received from Mars can undergo up to twenty-five separate filters and projections. The view that is received is a wide-angled fish-eye image that has to be turned into a linearized, or flat, version. Some radiometrically corrected images are created to increase the contrast between sky and ground and the individual features on the ground. One projection plots an x-y-z grid for terrain so that the teams can measure the distance of objects, the degree and direction of slopes, the amount of solar energy being received, and surface roughness.

One of the guys hands me the red-and-green glasses used in movie theaters to watch 3-D horror flicks, and suddenly I'm looking at an image of Mars in which I can see in glorious detail how much space is in between boulders. The people who drive the rovers have relied on the enhancement as a way to keep the rovers out of trouble for the extended mission. Our binocular vision and a host of evolved neurological responses allow us to mentally and unconsciously do the same as we walk around terra firma. For purposes of driving the rovers, JPL has to reply on VFX.

Deen and Alexander have made about two hundred panoramas from data sent back from *Spirit* so far, and they pull up the most recent one, which takes in a full 360 degrees near the summit of a hill. The picture is composed of ten images across, plus one down so we can see the tracks of the rover, and three more above for the sky. The software originally bracketed each of the shots with longer and shorter exposures, then picked the best ones to send. There is nothing remotely simultaneous about this view, which took several Martian days to capture.

This compiled view is yet another slow-motion parallel to how humans see in saccades. That is, we perpetually scan the scene in front of us in short arcs of observation, our attention alighting on various shapes in the order in which they appear important according to an evolved mental hierarchy. Although we assemble a scene from saccades within milliseconds, it still takes time. We don't see a scene all at once, as does a camera, but assemble it from multiple and separate visual fixations. The Mars panoramas are a crude and somewhat static version of the same process. And we scan the panorama with the same saccades that we use when looking at an actual landscape. Marscape. Whatever. We do the same in the movies, although the director is directing our vision as much as he or she is the cinematography.

Most of the Mars panoramas show variation in coloration from shot to shot, as they were taken at different times of day — and even on different days — and the angle of sunlight and dust load in the atmosphere change. Deen and Alexander usually minimize the differences to provide a consistent product, but they remind me that this is fundamentally different from computer graphics work. "Hollywood starts with a geometrical model that the artists try to make look real. We start with a real image." That was the thought I asked you to hold.

The images that we look at and that make Mars the "most real" are ones that capture our attention most rapidly and thoroughly. Our hereditary visual triage requires that we look at whatever is moving in a landscape before anything else, and that we figure out what it is, lest it come eat us. The most compelling views we have received from Mars are a sequence of three small images shot twenty seconds apart. The shots accidentally captured a dust devil moving across the surface of the planet at midday. Most pictures from off-world, from the moon to Jupiter, are stills, which don't show change. This relatively quick sequence animates the scene, the first time we've watched the atmosphere of a planet move in anything even approaching real time. The dust devil traverses from left to right across the field of vision, showing motion, hence change. Duration becomes visible. Time. We're spending time on Mars. I look at the sequence over and over again, almost unable to believe my eyes. It reminds me that it's often useful to consider *space* a noun, but *time* a verb. Mike Joyce would approve that it was an accident that captured apparently the most authentic images.

After spending a couple of hours showing me the panoramas, Guy Webster takes me back to ground level and we walk to an older building. Inside, we end up on a second-story walkway above the Mars sandbox. The stage is much smaller than the one at CPS, only 225 square feet versus 3,600, but it's large enough for people to learn how to drive on Mars by remote control. It's also where the engineers can solve traction problems on a controlled analogue of the Martian surface. Below us sits the third rover, about the size of a flattened golf cart and festooned with the same cameras, tools, and solar panels that bedeck the rovers on Mars.

The soil in this box is usually a mixture of red sandstone from Arizona and volcanic rock, which gives the correct texture as well as color for simulations of roving on Mars. Right now, however, the room features a white hillock made from sand used in playground sandboxes, dry clay mortar, and diatomaceous earth. This last material, which consists of fossilized microscopic shells from unicellular diatoms in the ocean, is so fine that people must strap on breathing masks when working with it. The reason for using this material is that it lubricates the sand and clay and makes a slippery slope equivalent to the ones inside a crater. The scientists wanted to explore the feature, and the engineers were pretty sure they could drive the rover down into the sloping pit, but getting it out was another matter. The third rover negotiated the dune in the sandbox without much of a problem, so they sent *Opportunity* down into the Martian crater. The vehicle toured about, found evidence of strata formed by water billions of years ago, then rolled painstakingly back out. Mission accomplished.

The walls around the sandbox are covered with incongruous military camouflage netting. The purpose is to give the cameras and computers sufficient visual complexity in the background, an illusion the engineers need to determine whether the cameras are functioning properly. JPL has played in several sandboxes, both indoors and outside. One of them is a large tilt-board containing six inches of sand for testing slopes of up to twenty degrees. At times the background of the sandboxes has been a painted backdrop of the Red Planet that looks like something out of a movie. To increase the likelihood that the rovers will survive what amounts to a crash landing on Mars, NASA sends its rovers to flat and relatively unscenic plains. The backdrops show what the public wants to see, the dramatic vertical relief of steeply eroded cliffs and mountains.

The IMAX film *Roving Mars* opened in theaters across the country in 2006. Parts of it were filmed in the sandboxes, and the director also used CG animation so that we could "see" the rovers as they perambulate about Mars. These special effects were then edited into sequences using the panoramas assembled by Alexander and Deen. It's no wonder that some conspiracy crackpots still insist that we don't really have rovers on Mars at all and that the Apollo missions to the moon were filmed on a Hollywood back lot. If I were skilled at either literary deconstruction or psychoanalysis, I would make something out of the exclamation by the director of JPL, Charles Elachi, shortly after the first rover had touched down: "Mars is now our sandbox, and we are ready to play and learn."

If sandboxes, whether on a playground or in the offices of a therapist, are places where individuals can be seen to exhibit behaviors that betray their inner concerns, I wonder what these two particular enclosures might reveal about matters that claim the attention of our society. Both Hollywood and JPL, that is, movies and space exploration, or art and science, use sandboxes as a virtual ground to manipulate things far away in time and space into our *presence,* or our *present,* words whose Latin root means "to be in front of." The CPS stage is used primarily and overtly for that purpose, but even the one at JPL feeds into the movie theater. Both serve to bring experiences far away in reality and imagination close to us so that we can experience and learn from them, although for different purposes. Hollywood is mostly after entertainment, although we can learn about history from some movies. JPL is chasing science objectives, although we can be entertained by its images. And in fact, every scientist knows how valuable entertainment from his or her research can be. Images that capture the public's imagination lead to votes for politicians who support funding for science.

It's not that the Mars sandbox and the re-creation of Wilshire Boulevard for *Volcano* and the French village at CPS were built for identical purposes, but they exist on a shared spectrum of activity and have a relationship to one another as analogous environments. Audiences will, in thrall to the moment, automatically privilege the narrative of each creation and accept the scenes as real—or at the very least, as realistic depictions—and not spend much time thinking about how it was done. We would benefit by occasionally countering this tendency to swallow unquestioningly these re-creations, to tease out the real from the unreal, and to understand when and where we are.

These visual manipulations bring places far away in time, space, and fantasy into what we experience as the here and now. Our deliberate diminishing of difference to bring the world within our grasp is the condition that I described in terms of a verb tense, the present perfect continuous. In film theory, critics talk about the endless moment of cinema, which is a version of eternity. Like verb tenses, this is not something I normally spend a lot of time thinking about, so I have relied on the work done by humanities scholar Eva Brann. She has written extensively on the history of how we think about time and, in particular, eternity. Of course, she cannot be blamed for how I've used her ideas.

We are said to live in the age of modernism, which is generally considered to have begun in France during the late nineteenth century as a revolt against the traditional, be it in art or science. In those terms, abstract art and quantum physics are seen as reactions against representational painting and Newtonian physics, for example. Tradition means knowledge handed to us from the past. The word *modern* comes from the Latin *modo,* "just now," which is another way of saying the present. It is not coincidental that cinema is a modernist medium and that studios say that they "present" a film to us. Modernism, as a state of mind, thrives on always "making it new" as it seeks to meet our addiction to stimulation. It lives in the present perfect continuous, which I propose is a verb tense of eternity.

The Roman philosopher and early Christian theologian Augustine wrote his *Confessions* in 399 AD, when he was forty-five, as a way of understanding the events that led him to convert to the still relatively new religion. In the tenth book of *Confessions,* he ponders how his memory of those events was formed, and then in the eleventh, the nature of time itself, wherein he makes the most well-worn statement about the subject ever made: "What, then, is time? If nobody asks me, I know. But if I want to explain it to the one who asked, I don't know." But Augustine, for all his modesty, also set out an idea about time that is strikingly familiar to modern physicists: that there is no time for us but the present. We experience the past only as memory, and the future only as expectation, for when the future arrives, it is, of course, the present.

Consider the clock. Any clock. As Brann points out, it measures only motion, whether it is that of a hand from second to second or that of a vibrating ion of mercury that shifts its position millions of times per second. Augustine came to the conclusion that time, as opposed to motion, is a stretching not of an external physical dimension, but of the mind, that is, the behavior of the brain: "So we must, properly speaking, not say: There are three times—past, present and future. But we should probably say, properly speaking: There are three times—a present of past things, a present of present things, a present of future things."

Stretch out the present enough, and you have what we call eternity. When we toss out the word *eternity* in conversation, we simply consider it the singular concept that embraces all time.

Brann, however, finds three kinds of eternity defined in her classical studies: Eternity is the "standing now" that timelessly embraces all time, whereas sempiternity is "current time in its endlessness." Thomas Aquinas, the thirteenth-century theologian who often quoted Augustine, posited yet a third kind of eternity in his *Summa Theologiae*, one that exists in between true eternity and time and which he called "aeviternity."

Brann parses the differences for aeviternity as follows: "It is not eternity because its beings are changeable, and it is not time because the change its beings undergo is not of their essence. It is the temporal place of beings that have in them some principle of change, but are indestructible, everlasting. These are the beings of fiction that love, but not in time and grow old, but do not age—the inhabitants of epics and novels." Entities in the aeviternal begin in time, but then go on to last forever. She calls it the temporal realm of angels, an appropriate name for the timescale of the primary product of the City of Angels.

Both what philosophers think about time and how physicists discuss it are sometimes different, sometimes not so different. In 1687, Newton described time as an absolute and unchanging dimension that contained an infinite number of instant moments from which one could deduce the motion of everything in the universe. Early in the twentieth century, however, Einstein demonstrated that time is relative to the position and motion of the viewer, an idea that, although it denies us the ability to produce clockwork predictions of the future, still relies on the notion that time consists of a series of instants. Peter Lynds, a young theoretician from New Zealand, caused an international controversy in 2003 when he proposed that such a thing as an instant is impossible, and that time consists only of intervals, which is what makes motion possible in the first place. This leads him to believe that time has no inherent direction and that time is nothing but the relative order of events. The idea disagrees with the cherished second law of thermodynamics (the basis for time's arrow), Einstein, Stephen Hawking, and about every other scientist on the planet. To call his idea controversial would be a grave understatement.

Where these ideas intersect with film is in how we mentally construct motion. Psychologists in the nineteenth century proposed that, when two slightly differing images are shown one right after another—say, that of a person walking, one photograph taken a second after the other—our retina retains an afterimage of the first photo, which then blends in with the second image to produce the illusion of motion. That theory, the so-called persistence of vision, supposedly explained why we see film that is shot and projected at 24 fps as continuous action. The theory gave way in 1912 to a series of experiments by Max Wertheimer, who showed that it was a matter of mental processing that produced the appearance of motion, not a physical blur in the eye. His observation, known as the *phi phenomenon*, was elaborated on by Hugo Munsterberg, who three years later proposed that the mind fills in the motion between the two images.

Current neurobiological research on how we perceive motion defines what happens in cinema as the phenomenon called *short-range apparent motion*. Remember that when we receive a very short-term stimulus, such as brushing up against something for less than 200 ms, we can't consciously perceive it. The event actually happened, and it was perceived, but the brain doesn't bring it into consciousness. It's not just a matter of how long it takes to process the input, but it's also part of the brain's triage, which demands that most sensory input be ignored in favor of things important enough to matter to survival.

A film that projects 24 fps in front of you is providing an image every 41.66 ms, well below the rate of conscious processing, and the mind copes by modeling the motion. It's not seeing actual motion, but creating apparent motion based on what it knows of how the world functions. As it turns out, our brain's optimal motion detection is for events we experience that last about 40 ms in duration. The parts of the brain that light up with electrical activity while we detect motion in the real world are the same parts that light up as we watch a film and as we dream.

In his second paper, Lynds went so far as to propose that the gap between what happens and our processing of it, a relationship of intervals caused by our neurological limitations, is a gap that forces our minds to construct the notions of time, motion, and physical continuity—what he calls flowing time and the progressive present moment. It alarms me when he notes that this process is "similar to that experienced when observing a continuous sequence of static movie frames in quick unison (commonly 24 frames per second), with no joins being observed." Alarming, because it seems that we are built for illusion and that we build to create an illusion of time.

After staring down into the sandbox at JPL and contemplating the relationships among philosophy, physics, and film, I have a headache. Webster walks me back to the reception center, where I take my leave. It's a hot summer day, and I'm remembering how cool it is at Forest Lawn among the tombs of the movie moguls. Perhaps it's time to go visit my great-grandmother again. After all, if ever I saw a concrete demonstration of faith in eternity and a manifestation of the present perfect continuous, it's in those flowers replaced every week in her crypt.

Just on a hunch, I swing by home first and collect the original deed to the property before heading to the memorial park. I'm glad I did. The woman sitting in the booth at the front door of the Great Mausoleum is at first quite friendly, but when I announce that I'm here to visit someone in the Sanctuary of Benediction, her eyebrows draw together and her lips purse. The man standing behind her and with whom she's been conversing leans in closer for a look.

"I'm sorry, but you'll have to give me some evidence that you're family," she says. I hand her the papers. Her eyebrows relax a fraction. "Oh, Mrs. Lyman. Well, that's quite all right, then." I smile and amble down the corridor, passing the large room with its reproduction of *The Last Supper*. The automatic narration and music are playing to an empty room, and in fact the only cars out front were those of the two staff people.

I find the little lever inside the first set of bronze gates and let myself in, then walk over to the crypt and open the second set. This time the flowers are variegated carnations. I sit on the bench in the nine-by-ten room, pull out my small notebook, and contemplate the two marble sarcophagi. In a few moments, I hear the blunted clicking of sturdy heels enter the sanctuary. The woman from the front desk walks casually past me, checks Jean Harlow's room next door, then leaves, carefully avoiding my eyes. I am, it appears, considered safely in the right place. I wonder how Great-Grandmother feels about being next to the starlet. I have no doubt Mrs. Lyman is attired in her customary long, black dress—as a child, I never saw her in anything else. Miss Harlow, dead from kidney failure at the age of twenty-six, is reputed to repose in her negligee. My own evocation of the present perfect continuous as a state of being makes me smile.

I sit and stare at the pale and heavy sarcophagi, one stacked above the other, and speculate about what my great-grandmother would have thought of us looking at pictures from Mars. She died before we even received pictures from the moon—she was born in 1860 and lived to be ninety-two. The year of her birth saw the first run of the Pony Express, which carried mail from St. Joseph, Missouri, to Sacramento, a distance of two thousand miles that the riders took ten days to cover. It was the year John Speke left to discover the source of the Nile above Lake Tanganyika, a body of water that he and Richard Burton had discovered only four years previously. And it was the year that Billy the Kid was born. The year she died, 1952, saw the atmospheric test of the first hydrogen bomb over Bikini Atoll and the introduction of Cheez Whiz. She was accustomed to change.

When I leave the cool recesses of the mausoleum, the matron at the door remarks how quiet it is, how few visitors there are, and that's the thought I take with me as I get into the car and drive uphill, deeper into the park. For all of the hundreds of thousands of people buried here, I see perhaps fifty cars total on the premises as I loop around the property. Most occupants of the cars appear to be Latino, a few look Asian in heritage. I see one white family, one African American man. The contract in my pocket from 1927 states: "Purchaser hereby certifies that he is of the white Caucasian race and that he will not inter or attempt to inter the body of any human being other than that of the white Caucasian race in said property." I would guess that, had Forest Lawn not changed the rules, it would have gone out of business.

I end up in a cul-de-sac I've never seen before at the far northeastern corner of the park, the pavement ending at the edge of a small hill about an acre in extent. "Memory Slope" is written on the curb. It's one of the few places where a residential neighborhood directly abuts the grounds, and I get out to walk around. Some of the plaques laid in the ground have birth dates in the 1880s, mostly for people who died in the 1950s. But one gravesite is guarded by a teddy bear and a handful of small toys. Another marker reveals that the body of a child who lived for only a single day was put to rest here last year.

I still hold my skepticism about the funeral business. A check of the recent price list at Forest Lawn reveals that to have your loved one cremated and to take home the ashes in a box costs around two thousand dollars, while a full-blown traditional burial in a walnut casket and a DVD tribute can run you more than thirty-five thousand. I think we should be buried virtually for free and our bodies used in service to the planet. I'd be much happier if my great-grandmother had been planted as fertilizer for a tree that I could climb, a tree that could be nurtured by family during life and after death. I can't imagine taking up space in her mausoleum. I'd rather be buried on Mars.

But cemeteries aren't going to go away, and neither are the movies, though both will no doubt continue to evolve. I'm looking for a way out of the impasse as I slowly pace among the bronze plaques set in the ground. Mary Pickford, Humphrey Bogart, Jimmy Stewart, and Walt Disney are among the stars buried here. But so are the bodies of writers such as Louis L'Amour, who wrote the frontier novels that helped create the genre of the Western. So are the remains of William Mulholland, the city engineer who built the Los Angeles Aqueduct and started a water war that's still going on, one of the largest conflicts over nature in the country. Aimee Semple McPherson is also interred here, the first televangelist (on radio, of course) and preacher in an automobile.

L'Amour and Mulholland and McPherson are as much members of the local pantheon in aeviternity as Clark Gable and W. C. Fields, other guests of Forest Lawn. The memorial parks can serve our purposes, can help us retain verb tenses other than the present perfect continuous by complicating our awareness of history, by making more tangible our past. When writing earlier about Forest Lawn, I suggested that schoolchildren should be taken on tours of infrastructure—things like oil fields and pipelines, the radio frequency forest atop Mount Wilson, and local cemeteries. Now I've convinced myself that this should be extended to all the public. Forest Lawn holds the largest concentration of entombed movie stars of any cemetery, but also a cross section of the local population as it has changed over the years. As I drive slowly back down the winding drive toward the bottom of the hill, I don't see any expensive German sheet metal up here. It's mostly clean but inexpensive Asian cars and a few older American sedans and pickups. It's families visiting their aunts and uncles and grandparents, the people who made the city run on a daily basis.

In the 1980s, the cultural critic and historian Norman Klein started to give walking tours of his neighborhood just west of downtown. He called them anti-tours, pedestrian narratives of places that no longer existed, which provided the basis for his book *The History of Forgetting: Los Angeles and the Erasure of Memory.* Klein uses neuroscience more as a metaphor than a factual background when he insists that to remember something is to simultaneously forget something else. But it's ultimately a useful literary notion, that we overwrite the past with

distractions in the present, movies among them. He counteracts
the forgetting by physically involving his students in the act of
remembering places and thus time. Jennifer Price, another Los
Angeles author, does the same thing when she gives tours of
the Los Angeles River. By necessity, segments of her trips are
conducted by car; after all, it's a long way from Canoga Park to
Long Beach. But at selected spots, her guests get out and walk
down into the channel to form their own memories.

Humans have externalized memory into place for as long in
the past as we are able to reconstruct. The Aborigines of Australia do it in their song lines (the basis of a walking practice),
as do the Apaches in Arizona with their morality tales tagged
to specific boulders, streams, ponds, and peaks. Los Angelenos,
because of our reliance on automobiles to conquer the decen-
tralized nature of our urban basins, have relinquished the discipline and need to reclaim this skill of memorialization. We need
to walk around and make stories out of everything, not just
what we take to be nature—the ocean and beaches and mountain parks—but also cell towers imitating a pine tree and the
concrete runoff channels used by mountains lions. We need to
think about not just the homes of the stars but also their graves,
and it shouldn't be seen as a ghoulish pastime to do so.

The plaques at Forest Lawn are placeholders. They represent matrices of places and memories woven into the lives of
people still living. The memorial park is a site where history
and nature have been brought together by design as a place to
be walked. I wouldn't know it from the few people I've seen
here when visiting, but a million people a year visit these lawns
and groves in Glendale. Forest Lawn doesn't currently allow
picnics, and that's a shame. The early cemeteries in America
did. Forest Lawn is as logical a place for a stroll and a midday

repast on the grass as are the lawns around the La Brea Tar Pits and the locations in Griffith Park where Gene Autry shot *The Phantom Empire.*

The Forest Lawn administration discourages people from hunting celebrity graves at its various facilities, an understandable position. But there's more to enjoy here than just the statuary, the mosaics of historical events, and the hilltop museum that's open and free to the public. The administration seems to understand this. In addition to displaying the coins and other items that Hubert Eaton collected, the galleries here and on the other Forest Lawn grounds offer small photography and painting exhibitions relevant to the residents—Latino history, the quest for water, and holy relics. The parks have the potential to become placeholders for the entire city, for our collective memories and not just individual ones. These communal places could encourage us toward both history and nature, as do the oil wells in the basin, the cell towers and telescopes, and the equestrians riding along the banks of the San Gabriel and Los Angeles rivers. And that would let us inhabit more than the present.

As I drive through the towering black iron gates and out to San Fernando Road, I roll down the windows, not wanting to use the air-conditioning. I'm driving, not walking, but I still want the temperature differential on my skin. It's worth a little sweat. I want to take my time, my own sweet time, getting home.

ACKNOWLEDGMENTS

Most of the books I write are about how human cognition transforms land into landscape. That's a process most easily observed in large and relatively empty spaces, such as the polar regions and other deserts, which are where my books tend to be set. So it came as a surprise one evening when Paul Yamazaki, the legendary book buyer for City Lights Bookstore in San Francisco, asked me when I was going to write a book about Los Angeles, an idea supported by our dinner companion, Rebecca Solnit. Two friends in Los Angeles later seconded the idea: Jennifer Price, who was then just beginning work on her own book about nature in the city, and Matt Coolidge from the Center for Land Use Interpretation.

Within a month, I began probing into the local petroleum industry, decided that the radio and television transmission towers punctuating our skyline should be looked at, and noticed on a hike that one of the Forest Lawn Memorial Parks sat next to a closed landfill. I was investigating, I realized, what we took out of and put into the ground, and what we broadcast through the air, all of which was relatively invisible except for the structures that represented the resources. At that point, the collective resonance of the topics seemed sufficiently dense for me to begin writing. As sometimes happens, however, my assumption about what I was trying to uncover—"invisible nature" in Los Angeles— shifted while I was working. Whenever I told people that I was writing about nature in Los Angeles, I received the same response that Jenny Price was getting as she worked on her essays: "What nature?" When I said the nature of the past, the corollary popped out: "What past? Los Angeles doesn't have a past."

In writing about cognition and landscape, I'm most often investigating the difficulties we have understanding the three dimensions of space in extreme environments such as the Mojave Desert and the Antarctic. But here in the city, it seemed the cognitive dissonance was more about time, the most invisible nature of all, although its effects are always and everywhere around us. While walking around the region to enlarge my awareness of space in Los Angeles, my sense of its past was also growing, and I found myself thinking as much about history as nature.

Among my discoveries was the realization that temporal issues are much more difficult to write about than spatial ones, physicists and philosophers alike unable to attain consensus within their disciplines about whether time exists as a separate dimension or as just a relationship among events. Neither are the scientists completely sure it has flowed at a constant rate during the 13.7-billion-year history of the universe—or if *flow* is even an applicable word. I find it comforting that we seem to have gotten no further in understanding it than Emerson, who wrote in his *Journal* on June 27, 1839: "Time dissipates to shining ether the solid angularity of facts." Including, presumably, the fact of its own existence.

I worked on these essays from late 1999 through early 2006. In the spring of 2002, I was a visiting scholar at the Getty Research Institute, in whose library I've been writing and conducting research ever since. My thanks to everyone at the GRI, but in particular Tom Crow and Charles Salas for their ongoing support. I was also a Hilliard Scholar at the University of Nevada, Reno, and twice a visiting writer with the Lannan Foundation in Marfa, Texas. In Reno, my friends and colleagues providing support included Bob Blesse, Michael Cohen, Cheryll Glotfelty, Alvin McLane, and Scott Slovic. For the residencies in Marfa, I owe my gratitude to Patrick Lannan, Martha Jessup, and Douglas Humble.

I would like to thank Hal Washburn and Reinhard Suchland of BreitBurn Energy for the first interviews I conducted in search of this book, and then, two years later, Paul Wieman, Robin Critchell, and Lu Rarogiewicz, who gave my son Mathew and me a tour around Mount Wilson. Wieman is a thirty-year veteran of broadcasting from the peak, and Critchell a CBS engineer who is a fount of local lore. Rarogiewicz not only runs the post office on the mountain, but also is the weather observer there for the National Oceanic and Atmospheric Administration, and a fount of information about the history of astronomy on the mountain. Several readers were also helpful in seeing this book completed. Tom Radko, Beth Hadas, and Matt Coolidge cast critical eyes on shaky premises and suspect facts. Patricia Boyd, as copy editor, was generous and diligent while correcting my lapses in logic and grammar. Errors I may have committed herein are, however, my own and not those of these informants, anyone listed in the sources at the end, or any other innocent bystanders.

The Los Angeles–area writers Jenny Price and D. J. Waldie were major inspirations for me not only to work on the book, but also to return to Los Angeles when it was time, as were my friends Denis Cosgrove, Jerry Moore, Larry and Ginny Kruger, and Ric and Mickey Hardman. Steve Aron at the Autry

National Center and Bill Deverell at the Huntington-USC Institute on California and the West helped expand my intellectual community here, and I remain in awe of their energies on behalf of our region.

After the writing, if one is lucky, comes the publishing. My agent, Victoria Shoemaker, is responsible for finding the right fit between manuscript and publisher, and my gratitude to her for bringing me together with the people I work with at Shoemaker & Hoard is immense. Those people include Jack Shoemaker, Roxy Font, Jill Kamada, Michelle Gray, and the designer Gerilyn Attebery. It's rare one gains a second family after turning fifty. I am, indeed, lucky. It makes me feel as if I have more time.

SOURCES

In listing the sources that have helped me think about Los Angeles, I am thanking—but also holding harmless for my mistakes—their authors.

LOS ANGELES AND ENVIRONS

The *Encyclopedia Britannica* (www.britannica.com) provided information on everything from methane and asphalt to the history of radios and antennae, and on burial practices and sanitary landfill technology.

Davis, Mike. *Ecology of Fear*. New York: Henry Holt and Company, 1998. Renowned earlier for his groundbreaking socioeconomic study of Los Angeles, *City of Quartz*, Davis advanced urban studies by analyzing civic culture squarely within the context of geography.

Klein, Norman. *The History of Forgetting: Los Angeles and the Erasure of Memory*. London: Verso, 1997. A somewhat eccentric but scholarly look at how the city's urban design policies, socioeconomics, and film industry conspire to erase local history.

Pitt, Leonard, and Dale Pitt. *Los Angeles A to Z: An Encyclopedia of the City and County*. Berkeley: University of California Press, 1997.

Robinson, John W. *Trails of the Angels: 100 Hikes in the San Gabriels*. Berkeley: Wilderness Press, 1998.

Schad, Jerry. *Afoot and Afield in Los Angeles County.* Berkeley: Wilderness Press, 1991.

Waldie, D. J. *Where We Are Now: Notes from Los Angeles.* Santa Monica, CA: Angel City Press, 2004. Like his first book, *Holy Land,* this is a series of poetic meditations that quietly take apart our assumptions about urbanism and suburbanism in the city.

COGNITION

Although it is not used as a specific source in this book, I recommend that readers interested in perusing more thoroughly how nature and culture come together in cities take a look at the anthology *Uncommon Ground: Rethinking the Human Place in Nature,* edited by William Cronon (New York: Norton, 1995). A seminal and controversial anthology on the topic, it developed out of a series of seminars held at the University of California at Irvine in 1994. Cronon's introduction is superb, and Jennifer Price's essay, "Looking for Nature at the Mall," a gem.

Allman, John. *Evolving Brains.* New York: Scientific American Library, 2000.

Anderson, Joseph, and Barbara Anderson. "The Myth of the Persistence of Vision Revisited." *Journal of Film and Video* 45, no. 1 (1993): 3–12.

Baker, Curtis L., Jr., and Oliver J. Braddick. "Temporal Properties of the Short-Range Process in Apparent Motion." *Perception* 14 (1985): 181–192.

Carter, Rita. *Mapping the Mind.* Berkeley: University of California Press, 1998.

Fauconnier, Gilles, and Mark Turner. *The Way We Think:*

Conceptual Blending and the Mind's Hidden Complexities. New York: Basic Books, 2002.

Libet, B., E. W. Wright Jr., B. Feinstein, and D. K. Pearl. "Subjective Referral of the Timing for a Conscious Sensory Experience: A Functional Role for the Somatosensory Specific Projection System in Man." *Brain* 102, no. 1 (March 1979): 193–224.

Lynds, Peter. "Subjective Perception of Time and a Progressive Present Moment: The Neurobiological Key to Unlocking Consciousness." Available on Peter Lynds home page, http://www.peterlynds.net.nz, 2003. Posted May 7, 2004.

Solso, Robert. *Cognition and the Visual Arts.* Cambridge: Massachusetts Institute of Technology Press, 1994.

Wilson, Robert A., Frank C. Keil, and Robert Anton Wilson, eds. *The MIT Encyclopedia of Cognitive Sciences.* Cambridge: Massachusetts Institute of Technology Press, 1999.

TIME

Blaise, Clark. *Time Lord: Sir Sandford Fleming and the Creation of Standard Time.* New York: Pantheon Books, 2000.

Browne, Malcolm W. "Refining the Art of Measurement." *New York Times*, March 20, 2001.

Deming, Alison Hawthorne. *The Monarchs.* Baton Rouge: Louisiana State University Press, 1997.

Weiner, Jonathan. *Time, Love, Memory.* New York: Alfred A. Knopf, 1999. A tour of the genes for a biomechanical basis of these three attributes, this is the source for many of my speculations on the biology of time. In no way should Mr. Weiner or the scientists he discusses be held accountable for my opinions.

TRACKING TAR

The La Brea Tar Pits are explained both on the walls at the George
C. Page Museum and through its online site (www.tarpits.
org). Text from the Web site can also be found in John M.
Harris and George T. Jefferson, eds., *Rancho La Brea: Treasures of the Tar Pits* (Los Angeles: Natural History Museum
of Los Angeles, 1985).

Benjamin Svetkey, "Lava Is a Many-Splendored Thing," *Entertainment Weekly*, April 25, 1997, provided details about the
making of *Volcano*.

Several publications from the California Department of
Conservation's Division of Oil, Gas, and Geothermal
Resources were helpful, including the *1998 Preliminary
Report of California Oil and Gas Production Statistics*
(Publication No. PR03, January 1999) and R. H. Samuelian, *South Lake Oil Field* (Publication No. TR32, 1984).
Readers interested in numerical details about the Salt Lake
Oil Field may wish to consult R. E. Crowder and R. A.
Johnson, "Recent Developments in Jade-Butress Area of
Salt Lake Oil Field," *Summary of Operations: California
Oil Fields* 49, no. 1 (1963).

Information on the potential hazards underneath the Belmont
Learning Center was gleaned from articles in the *Los Angeles Times*, in particular Doug Smith, "Belmont Hazards Are
Not Unique," November 25, 1999.

Alison Hawthorne Deming's astonishing sixty-poem sequence,
from which the experimental psychologist is quoted, is *The
Monarchs* (Baton Rouge: Louisiana University Press, 1997).

A TOUR OF THE ANTENNAE

Cleveland, Robert F., Jr., and Jerry L. Ulcek. *Questions and*

Answers About Biological Effects and Potential Hazards of Radiofrequency Electromagnetic Fields, OET Bulletin 56, 4th ed. (Washington, D.C.: Federal Communications Commission, Office of Engineering and Technology, August 1999). Frequently updated, this free (and online at FCC) publication gives an overview of the electromagnetic spectrum, the pertinent technology, and a thorough bibliography.

Fleishman, Glenn, and Stuart Luman. "State of the Spectrum," *Wired Magazine,* August 2001 (foldout on p. 77). A useful map of the electromagnetic spectrum from 30 MHz through 64 GHz.

Weschler, Lawrence. "L.A. Glows." *New Yorker,* February 23 and March 2, 1998.

LANDFILLING

Jacobs, Chip. "Landfills Being Recycled as Recreation Centers." *Los Angeles Times,* June 20, 2000.

Kaufman, Martin. "Recycling Yourself." *Earth Island Journal,* Summer 1999.

Newman, Judith. "At Your Disposal." *Harper's Magazine,* November 1997.

Sachs, Jessica Snyder. "At Play on a Field of Trash." *Discover,* June 1997.

Sloane, David Charles. *The Last Great Necessity: Cemeteries in American History.* Baltimore: Johns Hopkins University Press, 1991. This is an excellent overview of how cemeteries developed from church graveyards into rural parks during the nineteenth century and then into Forest Lawn Memorial Park in the early twentieth.

Worpole, Ken. *Last Landscapes: The Architecture of the Cemetery in the West.* London: Reaktion, 2003.

THE PRESENT PERFECT CONTINUOUS

Debord, Guy. *Society of the Spectacle.* Detroit: Black & Red, 1977. Other theorists, such as Baudrillard, have addressed the nature of time in a consumerist society, but I continue to find Debord the most useful and least bombastic.

Jonsson, Erik. *Inner Navigation.* New York: Scribner, 2002.

Kermode, Frank. *The Sense of an Ending: Studies in the Theory of Fiction.* London: Oxford University Press, 1967.

Roderick, Kevin. *The San Fernando Valley: America's Suburb.* Los Angeles: Los Angeles Times Books, 2001. A well-illustrated history of the valley by a local journalist. An online companion Web site, "The Valley Observed," is found at www.americassuburb.com.

MODEL BEHAVIOR

Basso, Keith. *Wisdom Sits in Places.* Albuquerque: University of New Mexico Press, 1996. This has become a classic in the study of memory, place, and narrative.

Brann, Eva T. H. *The Study of Time: Philosophical Truths and Human Consequences.* Eugene: University of Oregon Humanities Center, 1999. The author discusses the differences among time, eternity, sempiternity, and aeviternity.

Doane, Mary Ann. *The Emergence of Cinematic Time.* Cambridge, MA: Harvard University Press, 2002.

Fellman, Philip V., et al. "The Implications of Peter Lynds 'Time and Classical and Quantum Mechanics: Indeterminacy vs Discontinuity' for Mathematical Modeling."

Available at http://www.casos.cs.cmu.edu/events/conferences/ 2004/2004_proceedings/Lynds.v2doc.doc.

Kolker, R. P., and J. Ousley. "A Phenomenology of Cinematic Space and Time." *British Journal of Aesthetics* 13, no. 4 (Autumn 1974): 388–396.

Koppes, Clayton R. *JPL and the Amercan Space Program.* New Haven: Yale University Press, 1982.

William L. Fox has published poems, articles, reviews, and essays in more than seventy magazines, had fourteen collections of poetry published in three countries, and written ten nonfiction books about the relationships among art, cognition, and landscape. He was a visiting scholar in residence at the Getty Research Institute in Los Angeles, has twice been a Lannan Foundation writer-in-residence, and has been awarded fellowships from the Guggenheim Foundation and the National Endowment for the Humanities.

Fox was born in San Diego and attended Claremont McKenna College. He has edited several literary magazines and presses, among them the *West Coast Poetry Review*, and worked as a consulting editor for university presses, as well as being the former director of the poetry program at the Squaw Valley Community of Writers. In the visual arts, Fox has exhibited text works in more than two dozen group and solo exhibitions in seven countries, served as the Associate Director of the Nevada Museum of Art, and then as the visual arts and architecture critic for the *Reno Gazette-Journal*. In late 1979, he went to work at the Nevada Arts Council, first as the Coordinator of the Artists-in-Residence Program, then Deputy Director, and in 1984 Executive Director, a post he held until leaving in 1993 to write full time.